HIGHFIELD MANOR

Written by:

Angela Aspinwall

Cover illustration:

Andrea Pearlstein

To my husband, who faithfully encourages me to keep going.
I still feel the butterflies.

Highfield Manor

Chapter One

He felt like a child sitting here, waiting for someone to tell him what to do next. The only audible sounds were the raindrops on the stained glass windows and the rustling of papers. Stephen couldn't believe it had been a week since the death of his father, King George Henry Cavanaugh of Delmont.

Everything he knew to be constant in his life seemed to disappear with the king's passing. His sickness was long and painful, and he had known for many months that his father would never recover. They spent what little time he had left together in their summer home, Highfield Manor. The man trying to teach the boy his final lessons, and the boy trying to soak up the last memories he would ever have with the only family member he knew. Even with time to say goodbye, his passing was felt so greatly as to leave a large whole in the heart of the Prince.

He sat in the cushioned desk chair, his hands smoothed out on top of the ornate, mahogany desk. As he sat, patiently waiting, he pondered the mournful events over the last few weeks. Trying to stay strong, finding a way to let go, and willing himself to pretend it wasn't all just a show to hide his terror of being left behind. All his life, he felt afraid of people leaving him, and he had no idea why. His mother had died when he was a small boy, but he was far too young to remember. What had created this fear of abandonment? What had stirred this desperation inside of him? Maybe he was simply broken. Maybe he couldn't do this alone. How would a broken man lead a kingdom? How would he face the trials of his people when he knew so little about the demons of his own life?

What would happen now? He knew the answer but he still wished someone was left for him to ask the question. He was all alone now, the last of his bloodline. No family.

Well, that wasn't entirely true. He had Garrett. His hired companion, since he was 8. Thirteen years later, Garrett had long ago become his best friend. He had a passion for life and a love for people that Stephen didn't want to be away from. Now that Stephen had to take the thrown, Garrett would no longer be employed by the castle, and he would go away too. Stephen could hire an advisor for a while until he felt ready to run the kingdom himself, but he had known for a long time that Garrett wanted to make his own life. Garrett wanted to be part of the village in which he lived before coming to the castle. If only Stephen could find a way to keep him living here. He was running out of reasons to ask him to stay.

Sitting in his father's office, preparing to hear his father's final wishes, he had never felt so isolated.

A year ago, almost to the day, he recalled sitting outside of the king's bedroom, waiting for news from the doctor. He had been growing weaker for some time now, but his father kept brushing it off, saying he was not a young man anymore. For a while, they were happy to believe that. It was when the swelling in his legs started that Stephen knew something more serious was going on. Perhaps he just needed some rest.

They could slow down for a while, at least until he was better. He *would* get better, of course.

The door opened and the doctor stepped out, closing it behind him. He seemed deeply troubled, his face, grim. Stephen stood up quickly and tried to brace himself for what he was about to say.

"Your Majesty," the doctor began.

The prince interrupted, "Please doctor, how is he?"

The doctor looked disheartened. "Did your father ever tell you about the time when he had Scarlett Fever?"

Is that all this was? "Yes, after my mother died. He was coming home from a trip, I think."

The doctor nodded his head sadly. "Sometimes, when people get very sick, it leaves something behind that can affect them later in life. I understand he has been especially tired as of late, probably much more than he lets on, and the swelling…"

The hesitation from the doctor was almost more than the prince could stand. He just wanted to know he would be alright. "Please, sir, just tell me."

The doctor shook his head in defeat. "It's his heart, its failing. I am so sorry. I don't know how much time he has left. Months, perhaps a year. All we can do now is keep him comfortable..."

Back in the present, a knock at the door alerted him that it was time. Magistrate Phillips was coming with some documents that the king requested he see after his death. Stephen braced himself, shook off the emotions that threatened to cloud his judgement, and opened the door.

"Good morning, your highness," he tipped his hat before removing it and waited to be invited into the room. He was an older man, much shorter than Stephen, his voice timid. "How are you today?"

Stephen opened the door wider and asked the man inside. "Very good magistrate, thank you. Please sit down." Extending an arm to point toward the chair opposite his father's desk, he wondered if he was doing a good enough job of hiding his pain.

Magistrate Phillips nodded and took the seat that was offered. He looked uncomfortable, not knowing what to say to his future king. They both sat in silence for a moment. "Shall we begin, sir?"

Stephen nodded his head once and sat forward in his seat.

"I have been instructed to give you this letter in the event of your father's death. I understand it contains a very delicate secret he was not prepared to share until after his passing."

"A secret?" he looked at the magistrate in disbelief. There were no secrets between present and future king. They had known for a year that it would be the kings last, they spent the entire time preparing, sharing information, and saying goodbye. There wasn't even a hint of this dark secret that seemed to contain some measure of regret. He tried to understand as he read it out loud.

"My son,

If you are reading this, it means that I have passed. You loved me so well, and saw so little fault in me, that I was never brave enough to tell you this before. I'm sorry, son. Sorry that I've left you, and sorry that you have to find out the mistakes I've made like this.

I loved your dear mother very much. She was my whole world. When she passed away and left us both, I was lost. I eventually found solace with you, Stephen, as I should have from the start. But in my grief, I wrongly attempted to find comfort in going away from the home where my wife took her last breath.

I traveled to the other side of the country and spent some time with a woman I met there, named Mary. She resembled your mother, both in appearance and spirit. Of course, when she learned who I was, she encouraged me to return to my kingdom and my son. While I came back ready to embrace life again, I never stopped regretting my actions with Mary. It was not the actions of a good king, a good father, or a good man. I spent the rest of my life trying to mold you to become better in every way than myself.

Forgive me, son, I tell you this in hopes that you will not make the same mistakes in your grief for me.

When I knew I was near the end, I attempted to find Mary. I wanted to apologize before my death, and see to it that she would live comfortably for the rest of her life. I discovered that she died several years after we had met, and had left behind a daughter.

She is your half-sister, Stephen. Until recently, I swear I had no idea of her existence. I wish I had gotten enough time to meet her, to bring her here and show her the love I would have given her if I had only known. She knows nothing of us or her birthright. It is my last wish that she would. Please make this right, for all of us.

Your loving father."

So many emotions entered his mind. Shock, confusion, disbelief.

Hope.

"A sister? I have a sister?"

Magistrate Phillips looked just as shocked, not having read the letter previously. "It…it appears so, your majesty."

"I can't believe it. I…" Stephen didn't know what to think, what questions to ask first. "Where is she? What's her name?"

The magistrate rummaged quickly through the papers he had brought, trying to find any information that would answer his questions. He then looked at the letter in the prince's hand and noticed a few scribbled notes on the back. "There, sir." He pointed to it.

Stephen quickly turned the letter over and read the notes. It was the name and location of the girl, and the fact that she was placed in service after the death of her mother. "Elise" Stephen whispered. Then, looking up at him, "Mournstead, I am not familiar with this village, do you know it?"

"I believe so, sir. A small town to the east, 3 or 4 days ride, somewhere around here." He pointed it out on a map. "Best to keep this to yourself until you know how the girl will react, the part of the country he is referring to is very poor. The girl will know almost nothing about the kingdom."

Stephen took a moment to process what was happening. A week ago, he lost his father. Now, somewhere in the world, a piece of him remained. He didn't care if this girl was homeless, or mad, or poor. She was his father's daughter and that's all that mattered.

"I have to meet her." He announced with determination. "Whoever she is, wherever she may come from, she is family. My family. I will make this right, for her and for my father." He hesitated for a moment before adding, "Tell no one of this."

The next day, Stephen sent for the royal guards. He instructed them to locate this village, find the girl in question, and do whatever they needed to do to bring her back to Highfield Manor. He entrusted to them a large sum to release her from servitude, and ordered a carriage to accompany them. They were puzzled by such an odd request, but prepared to obey. And what were they to tell this girl?

"Simply that, her king has died, the surviving prince has found a distant relation to her, and extends an invitation for her to come to the palace."

The leader of the guards nodded. "To visit, sir?"

Stephen was quick to reply. "To stay."

With that he dismissed them, and bid them farewell on their quest. They knew it would take some time to find this small village and the girl, and that the trip back would be even slower as to make the journey comfortable for her.

Several days later, Garrett found Stephen sitting alone in the courtyard, staring into nothingness, seemingly taken over by pain and sadness. When he approached him, he found him deep in thought, but with a face full of something different than the grief he had been wearing the last few weeks. Something between contentment and fear. He couldn't place it.

The prince, at the age of twenty one, already had all the appearance and demeanor of a king. His short, well-kept blond hair and his clear, insightful blue eyes commanded respect. Taller than his father was, in perfect physical condition, he appeared to fit the mold of the leader of his people. Prepared for nothing else, he was well suited, able, and more than willing to take the thrown. Garrett felt less useful to the prince with each passing day. He tried to find his passion elsewhere in preparation for the day he would be sent away, but his heart was here. This was his home, where he had spent most of and the best part of his life. His job was easy, natural. With the title of companion he had very quickly become a genuine friend to his master.

The two were the same age, but that was the only similarity between them. Garrett was taller, broader, and more muscular than his friend. He had loose dark brown hair that fell naturally on his head. Large, dark brown eyes that saw beauty in everything and everyone. He had a way of making people feel special the moment they met him.

While Stephen cared about rules, Garrett cared about justice. Stephen did things meticulously, with great planning and preparation, but Garrett accomplished much with passion and persistence.

"Someone is due to arrive at the castle soon, Garrett. Someone I have never met, but who I will try to turn into a princess." He seemed to speak without any emotion, numb to the rest of the world. Garrett didn't know if he was serious.

He waited silently for a few moments, thinking there must be an explanation. Afraid to say the wrong thing, he had kept his distance lately. "I miss your father too, Stephen. He was the closest thing to a father I have had in a long time. I know you will fill his shoes better than he ever hoped. But guests? Now? Are you sure you are ready to entertain?"

Stephen tried to explain without revealing too much. He trusted Garrett with his life and wanted to share this burden with him, but what if this girl didn't want the title? If that happened, he would help her leave gracefully, set her up well for the rest of her life, and no one needed to know of his father's deepest regret. "She isn't a guest, exactly. She is a country girl, found to share a very distant bloodline with me and I have been advised to prepare her for royalty." He watched his friend carefully, knowing he was one of the only people alive that could catch him in a lie. It was truth, in part, and he hoped that would be enough to keep him from digging deeper.

"I see," he told his friend. "I'm sorry you have been asked to do this so soon. I will help in any way I can." Garrett grieved with his friend, he was hurt and lost and lonely. He knew someday soon he would be sent away and he saw this as an opportunity to be made useful. He wished he had a reason to stay, but once Stephen took the crown, he knew his job would be over.

Stephen's numb state broke to reveal a moment of peace. "Thank you, my friend."

As the following weeks passed, Stephen left his usual place of grief to take up a new obsession. Trying to remember how his father had prepared for distinguished guests, he took every measure to ready his staff and the Manor. Each room was picked over with a fine-toothed comb, rugs swept, hearths cleared, linens washed, and windowsills dusted. He could be found at all hours of the day either inspecting or ordering something to be cleaned. There was not a single servant who he did not speak with concerning instructions and accommodations. But what was he preparing for? What would his sister need? "Probably nothing that I am doing," he thought to himself. Still, he had to do something. Anything was better than the pain of knowing he was alone. He was surrounded by people every day, but those people were afraid to talk to him, spend any real time with him, as if he were made of glass and would break at the slightest touch.

Garrett, his most trusted and valued friend, had kept an unusual distance since the King's death. Was he counting the days until he could leave? Was that all their friendship had amounted to? They used to be like brothers, now, they were almost strangers. Stephen was hurting and Garrett didn't seem to care at all. Suddenly, a mischievous idea crossed his mind, and he walked quickly toward Garrett's room down the hall.

He instructed a few of his servants to follow him and then knocked at Garrett's door.

Garrett walked over to the door and opened it, finding Stephen and two maids. This was an unexpected and unusual visit, and he couldn't imagine the purpose. They all stood at the doorway without saying a word; Stephen, with his sly plan, Garrett, not making sense of what he was seeing, and the maids, knowing what was coming and that it wouldn't end well.

"Yes?"

Stephen smiled, almost gleefully. "Your turn" he announced. He waited for his friend to put the pieces together. Maybe this was the only way he would get to spend some time with him.

Realization suddenly hit and Garrett put both hands on the door to close it. Stephen anticipated this move and put a shoulder to the door to keep it open.

"Oh no, not this room, don't you dare!" Garrett spoke forcefully, his tone increasing as he pushed at the door to close it.

"Come on, Garrett, all the other rooms are done, except this one!" Stephen put more effort than what he thought he should have to keep the door from closing. "Wouldn't it be nice to have a clean room?!"

"It's clean enough for me!" He remembered the newcomer and added, "She won't even see this room, Stephen…"

The prince's eyes brightened at this unusual turn of excitement, but he was losing the battle of strength with the door. He knew Garrett was stronger. "You never know! Besides, this way we will know everything is ready!"

Garrett gave a final push and the door closed, hard. "My room, Stephen! Go clean somewhere else!"

Stephen sighed in defeat. "Alright, fine, have it your way, live in filth!"

Garrett gave an exasperated, "Thank you!" and stepped back from the door. No way was he going to let the prince have his way in this room. It was filled with memories of the life they had shared. Stephen may be ready to let it go, but he wasn't yet.

Stephen dismissed the maids and turned back toward his office. "Well, that was fun," he thought whimsically to himself. He tried to picture Garrett, mortified as each item was picked up for inspection. He knew he wouldn't let him in, but it was fun to try. For just a few moments, when Garrett was speaking to him in an unguarded manner, the world made sense again, and someone was talking to him without walking on eggshells. It always made him feel better to talk to his friend, even if it was just for a brief moment.

This gave Stephen an idea. Walking back toward Garrett's room, he stopped at the door just before it. Turning the handle and looking inside, he remembered something from his childhood. Quietly, he stepped inside the closet, and listened.

Many years ago, when they were just boys, a game of hide and seek was played. It had rained for so long, and they were so bored of being cooped up inside that one of the maids suggested it to keep them out of trouble.

"No Stephen, you aren't allowed to hide in my room, it's too easy for me to find you!" The boy commanded.

"But this house is so big, what if I get lost?" was the innocent reply. It was the first time the king had left them with just the servants for the day at Highfield.

Garrett rolled his eyes at the thought of the prince getting lost in his own manor. "I'm going to count again, and this time, go somewhere else! One…two...three…"

Stephen ran out of the room and looked down the large hallway. His heart raced as Garrett counted and he knew he had to hide quickly. As quietly as possible, he opened the door of the very next room, climbed into the closet, and waited. As his breathing grew calmer, he noticed he could hear Garrett's voice through the wall. "Thirty seven…thirty eight…thirty nine…"

Garrett finished counting and looked throughout the room. After a few minutes, he realized Stephen had finally hid somewhere else, and he went into the hallway, pleased with the thrill of the hunt. Stephen heard him leave and walk down the hallway in the opposite direction of where he was hidden. He waited until he could no longer hear any movement, then quietly slipped right back into Garrett's room to play. An hour later, an exasperated boy entered the room, tired and frustrated at not finding his friend. Thinking the prince must have been in here all along, he declared that he no longer liked the game, and they played with wooden boats for the rest of the day.

Stephen never told his friend how easily he could hear him from that room, and now he was glad of it. If his best friend could hear the newcomer, it might help him keep a closer watch over her, just in case. He told the maids to prepare this room for the new arrival.

Chapter Two

Elise sat crying in the carriage, just moments away from her new home. She held her one bag, containing everything on this earth she could call her own. A comb, a tattered book, and her mother's necklace, broken and tied in her father's handkerchief. She never knew her father and didn't remember much of her mother. She spent six years going from house to house, until being put into service at the age of eleven. She had watched children, cleaned every size home, prepared every dish, and tolerated the usual treatment of a lowly, orphaned servant girl. Her last establishment was with a drunkard, Mr. Devlin, who grew more violent with each emptied bottle. She had broken a cup while cleaning, and if the royal guard hadn't arrived at just that moment, she may not be alive today. They paid the man what a new servant would cost him and told her to pack her things. Not waiting for an explanation, she quickly obeyed.

Once she was safely in the carriage, she was very briefly told the same thing that Stephen told Garrett. That she was found to be a distant relative in the royal bloodline, and with the death of the king, they needed her to come to the Manor.

The royal family had spent the last year at their summer home, Highfield Manor, in the village of Westmore. It was a large and stately home in the countryside. This ensured that the king could spend the rest of his time quietly; the royal castle of Delmont would have been too much for his health and had been closed off. She was told the Prince would not reside in it until he took a wife or the thrown. She hoped that was not what they were bringing her there for. While she was very happy to be taken from a place where she knew nothing but sadness, she did not want to be taken from a prison of servitude to a prison of forced marriage.

The driver announced their impending arrival at the Manor grounds. Suddenly, Elise was very aware of her horrendous appearance. Her hair was tangled and unkempt, her clothes were thin and torn, and her hands and nails dirty from the last chore that almost took her life. Reaching softly to her face, she took notice of the hot cheeks from crying, the many tender spots where bruises were, and small marks along her jawline the size of fingernails. Wincing, she lowered her hands back down to the carriage seat, feeling defeated, and lifeless. What could she possibly have to offer the people who lived here?

She had spent many days traveling with the royal guards. They tried to offer any assistance she needed, but she was far too afraid to accept. They stopped each night at various inns, and she was told to try and sleep. She tried to eat, tried to think. Most of the time she just hid in the corner of her room, fearing that evil man would find her. Each morning when it was time to get back into the carriage, she felt a little safer, knowing they were going further and further away from him.

Elise picked up the comb and desperately tried to tame her wild tresses. Suddenly, she both heard and felt a loud "snap". Her comb had crumbled under the stress of her tangles and was now nothing more than a useless, broken, and shattered thing. "Just like me," she said to herself. Elise gathered the fragmented comb back into her bag and tied it shut.

The carriage stopped and she took a deep breath, dried her tears and picked up her small bag. She was already so afraid of people, and so unaccustomed to speaking to them, that she had no idea how she would get through the day.

Stephen was waiting patiently at the entrance with the customary set of staff to greet the newcomer. Garrett stood just behind him at his right, knowing there was something Stephen wasn't telling him, but also knowing not to pry while his friend was in such a state of grief. He was willing to do everything he could to help his friend through this time.

Both men had no idea what to expect when the carriage stopped.

Elise stepped out, slowly, cautiously. She was timid, scared, and looked very out of place. The gentlemen were half expecting a wild girl, and while her initial appearance spoke loudly of neglect and abuse, they saw a beautiful woman. Through her ragged clothes they could see a slim figure, tall and lovely. Long dark hair, the same clear blue eyes as her brother. Stephen's father had mentioned in his letter that Elise's mother resembled his own, and he saw plainly that it was true. Between Mary's resemblance of the queen and the fact that her father was the king, she looked every bit as part of the royal family as he did. The only part of her that differed was the darker hair. It looked more the color of Garrett's. He turned to see his friends' reaction, and he was not disappointed.

Garrett stared at her, focused and intent. This woman, looking as though she would much rather bury her head in the sand than be standing before them, was the most beautiful girl he had ever seen. Her timidity made his heart ache. She looked just as lost and lonely as he felt he would be when his time came to leave.

"Welcome to the castle, Elise. I am Stephen Cavanaugh, Prince of Delmont, son of the Late King. This is my companion and right arm, Garrett Hennessy." Her eyes showed little more than fear. Never having been addressed in this way, she had no idea how to respond. She looked first at Stephen, some distant cousin perhaps. She recognized herself in him and knew instantly that this was all real. How could it not be, they could pass for siblings. She looked at the ground for a moment, drew breath again and brought her eyes to Garrett. Her cheeks burned red at the sight of him, how handsome he was. How could she learn to be a princess and live in this house with the future king and his incredibly handsome right hand man?

She barely whispered her thanks before her eyes went dark and her legs went out from under her.

Elise woke up in a soft bed with silk blankets. She was surrounded by luxury and felt as though her slightest movement might damage something. Slowly, she turned her eyes and looked about the room. It was large and ornate. The bed posts looked like gold, and there was more finery in this one room than she had ever dreamed of in her life. Suddenly, she felt so small and out of place in this room fit for a princess. Remembering where she was, she tried to rise. Elise got halfway up when her head started to get fuzzy, and she anticipated the fall back into bed when a pair of strong arms caught her.

"Steady now, nice and easy" Garrett said softly as he easily placed her back on the bed. She hadn't seen him in the corner chair, ready to answer her questions privately, sensing her fears and unease. When she woke up, she looked so lovely that he was unable to speak. Thankfully he moved fast enough to catch her before she fell.

Elise didn't know what to think or say to this kind man who stood before her. She spoke very quietly, completely unsure of herself and her situation. Touching her forehead, she tried to clear her mind enough to remember his name. "Thank you, Mr… Hennessy, is it?

"Please," he said kindly, "call me Garrett."

"Garrett" she repeated. It was a good, strong name, and, judging by the looks of him, she suspected it was fitting to its owner.

He bowed slightly and smiled. "It's very nice to meet you."

She smiled back at him, and he returned to his seat.

"I didn't know how you took your tea, so I had them bring a tray." He had so many questions, ones he knew she couldn't answer, but he wished he could ask. Was she there to marry his friend? Was it his job to help her get used to royal life? Would that be his final task?

And, from somewhere deep within his soul, he wondered, how could he get her to fall into his arms again?

"I've never been served tea before" was her weak reply. Being surrounded by luxury while handsome men served you? If she could just learn to breathe again, she just might like it here.

They spoke easily for the next several minutes, she asked simple questions and he tried to answer her without asking too many of his own.

"How long have you lived here?" She began.

"I've been with the family thirteen years. We usually just spend summers here, and live at the castle the rest of the time, but we've spent the entire last year here."

She mentioned that the guards had told her a little about that as well. "Who is at the castle, now?"

"Most of the staff stay behind when we come here, Stephen takes day trips a few times a week to handle any pressing issues, and a messenger brings reports and handles correspondences daily."

Elise took in this new information and tried to think of more questions to ask, preparing herself. When she couldn't think of any, Garrett offered some tips.

"Our housekeeper's name is Hazel, she and Olivia will be able to help you with anything you need. Feel free to roam about, we are not so formal here."

This brought her some comfort. If they were at leisure in this place, it would be easier to adjust. Knowing Garrett was also in service, albeit in a very different way, made her feel much more comfortable than talking to a royal prince.

When their tea was gone, he took his leave. He found himself wanting to stay, but he wasn't quite sure why.

"What is wrong with me?" Garrett said to himself on his way to Stephen's office. It's not like he had never seen a woman before. He could think of 10 other women he knew from the village. All of them, lovely. Any of them, more than happy to be his. He couldn't recall any of their names, for some reason. There wasn't anything special about Elise to make him feel like this. Nothing fancy in her eyes; those eyes, so blue and clear and vibrant.

Maybe there was. But this girl could very well be intended for his best friend. No matter how he felt, he wouldn't stand in the way of that.

He just wouldn't.

Reaching Stephen's office, he briefly knocked on the door before entering, knowing he was expected.

"How is she?" Stephen asked, looking up from his desk with curiosity.

"Alright, I think. Nervous, shy. She seems like she doesn't know what to say or do." Garrett answered.

Stephen nodded his head absent-mindedly, "I'm sure she is. That's to be expected."

"What do you know about her?" Garrett wondered if now his friend wanted to disclose the missing pieces he was keeping to himself.

The prince walked up to the window and looked out onto Garrett's stables before answering. Three years ago, he began to realize that his friend needed something to do while he was attending the castle with his father. He knew Garrett was a natural with the royal horses, and he wanted to encourage him. Giving him the manor stables and letting him pick any horses he wanted was a small price to pay to keep Garrett's interests in staying with the family, at least for a little while. His friend proved to be a natural trainer to the large, lively animals. Spending much of his free time with them, he found comfort during this time of grief and uncertainty. Stephen wished he had something to draw comfort from right now.

"Not very much. She was orphaned when she was around five, went from house to house until going into service when she was still a child. When my guards found her, she was in a bad situation, violent. When they told her where they were taking her, she didn't hesitate to leave. Didn't ask any questions, didn't care where she was going."

"Just wanted to get out" Garrett perceived.

Stephen nodded. "I think so too. She is so used to following orders and being overlooked, it's no wonder she fainted in the presence of so many people welcoming her."

"What do you intend to do with her?" Garret didn't mean for the question to come out so fast.

"For now, nothing. Let's give her a few days to get used to being here, being waited on for a change. Let's see how she gets on before deciding on the next step."

With that, Garrett gave him a slight nod and went out. He needed some time to process this change, to think about the future, his future.

Stephen returned to his desk and began to open the letters that were brought in earlier that day. He stopped short when he saw the one from a neighboring country. Opening it, he read the letter with a mixture of puzzlement and delight. It was from King Frances, inviting him to visit his kingdom and stay at the palace. Stephen was surprised to receive an invitation so soon after meeting the King's daughter, Christina, but he couldn't wait to answer it with affirmation. A visit with her was exactly what he had been hoping for. They had met at his father's funeral, and he felt like they had missed out on something that could have easily been between them had it not been for the circumstance. She must have felt it, too. It was a spark that no one else in the world noticed, not even Garrett, but it had replaced a tiny part of the sadness of that day with a little bit of hope.

Christina's soft blonde curls came to his mind, her easy and pleasant manners, and the effortless way she commanded a room. His pen stopped short as he realized how happy he was feeling. Perhaps it wasn't right for him to have a moment of happiness in the midst of his loss? What would his Father think? What would his future people think? He considered declining the invitation, and then felt worse than before. Maybe he could go, just for a few days. Maybe nothing would even come of this, after all. He decided not to tell anyone where he was going, or why. It just seemed…easier that way. He finished his letter and sent it away.

Elise walked about her new room, sipping her second cup of tea, and thinking about the men she now shared a home with. What were they like? Did they take to drinking? Women? Violence? They seemed so nice, surely royalty would treat her better, as they already had. She had never met with such politeness, never attended to, she barely remembered anyone being so kind to her. Just the quiet afternoon spent in her own room seemed like such a luxury. She lightly touched a brush on the dressing table when someone knocked on her door. She jumped back, fearing punishment for touching the beautiful things. To her surprise, two maids entered her room. Were they here to instruct her on her duties? Is that what she was here for?

"Good afternoon, Miss," the older of the two addressed her with a warm and welcoming smile, "My name is Hazel, and this is Olivia," gesturing to the younger woman, "I am the housekeeper, and Olivia is one of our finest maids. We are here to help you dress."

They had several bundles in their arms. Never having help to dress before, she wondered how many things one girl needed. She looked down at her tattered dress and felt very grateful that she would be made presentable to the two young men. Olivia went into the adjoining room to prepare a bath while Hazel tried to help her feel more comfortable. She gently brushed out Elise's hair in front of a large, ornate mirror and asked her a few simple questions about her life.

"My master has told me not to expect much conversation from you, Miss, but I can see behind those shy eyes that you could use a friend." Hazel was very kind, she set Elise at ease quickly and easily. She told her about the many homes she had lived in, and the many things she was expected to do while in service.

"I once lived in a home with a young mother, Grace. She needed help with her new baby and I was to care for him while she rested. He was such a sweet baby. I liked it there." Hazel brushed out her hair so softly that it was almost like being comforted by her own mother's gentle touch. "Most of the homes, I did not like. They were…not kind to me." Elise looked down at the floor. "The last one, he wanted……more from me than I wanted to give."

Hazel clicked her tongue. "There is none of that here, I can assure you. Prince Stephen wouldn't stand for it. He is a very good master to us. His father, bless him, taught him well. He is despondent at this time, but it is to be expected. I think you are just what he needs to stir him up again."

Elise's cheeks burned at the innocent comment. Was she meant to romance this prince? She knew it was common for royalty to marry cousins, but she barely knew him. He seemed so sad, she would try to do what he asked, but she hoped it wasn't that.

Without warning, Garrett came to her mind. He was so kind, so strong. His own sadness seemed to be used to help those around him. She felt comforted by his presence. She was glad to have a friend in this house.

Olivia emerged from the adjoining room. "Your bath is ready, Ma'am."

Elise walked quietly into the room but didn't know what to think when she entered. Several candles had been lit around a large tub. It was so big it could fit her entire body, with room to spare. It was filled with sweet smelling, hot water. She had never had such a bath. Hazel showed her the various soaps and the two maids washed out her long hair. After she was clean, a set of warm, fluffy towels wrapped around her. Olivia set new undergarments behind a dressing screen and directed her to change. Elise dried herself and slipped into the silky things with awe. Never had such fine clothing so much as touched her skin before.

"When you are ready, we have a dress to help you into." Hazel announced.

Elise sheepishly came out from behind the screen and saw the most beautiful dress pieces. They were ivory colored, the skirt so long that it touched the ground. Once it was fastened to her, she reveled in how well it fit her form. Just tight enough to show her curves, and it flowed from the bodice with such grace. Tiny, detailed embroidery work decorated the top and bottom. She felt both wonderful and foreign in this regal attire.

"This will have to do until we can fit you to your own gowns." Hazel said as she led Elise to the mirror. When she saw her reflection, she gasped. She saw herself like never before. The simple ivory gown was stunning. Her clean, rose scented skin glowed, and her long, flowing hair glistened. She placed her feet in the softest slippers that fit her perfectly. It was as if she were in a dream, but her dreams were nowhere near this fine. "Until then, the queen's old things do fit you nicely."

"The queen?!" Elise stepped back, suddenly feeling like a thief in stolen garments. "I didn't realize, oh I couldn't possibly…"

Hazel laid her hands gently on Elise shoulders and smiled. "You can and you will, Miss. These things have not been used in 20 years, Prince Stephen has never even seen any of them. He wanted them to be made useful to you. You get to look like a princess now, after all."

Elise stood back in front of the mirror, trying to picture herself as Stephen wanted her to be. "A princess" she whispered, "what do I know of such things?"

"You will learn, in time." Hazel had been with the family since she was a girl of fifteen. The queen had died five years later. She was the only servant in the castle that had been with the family long enough to guess who Elise really was. She wouldn't share her suspicion, but she would do everything in her power to help Elise embrace her birthright.

Someone knocked at the door to announce dinner had been served.

Hazel looked at Elise, squeezed her hand, and smiled. "Are you ready?"

Elise looked once more at the reflection in the mirror of this new person she had to try to become. "Yes."

She lied.

Chapter Three

Elise was lead to the formal dining room, used tonight in her honor. There must have been a hundred candles lit. The room was massive, impressive. The mahogany table had lion sized claw feet, and the 20 or 30 gold chairs were cushioned in deep red velvet. Two chandeliers, covered in crystals, hung fearfully at the ceiling. Fit for true royalty, and terrifying. For a girl who had lived her entire life in the shadows, she had no idea how to behave in the spotlight. "Do not faint," she said wordlessly to herself over and over as she made her way through the room.

Garrett couldn't believe the transformation. This lowly servant girl was stripped of her past life and had become a vision of grace and beauty. Her deep brown hair looked like silk as it flowed down her back in large, elegant strands, and that dress, it fit her perfectly. Every curve he didn't notice before was brought to light. He pictured wrapping his arms around her and looking into her beautiful eyes. She looked the part, indeed. Everything he wanted for…..

……his friend? Yes, that's right. Stephen. She was brought here for Stephen. He shook his head to try to clear his mind.

The two men immediately stood at her entrance, which made Elise freeze. Why were they standing? She wondered. Did she do something wrong? It must be her dress. She knew wearing the queen's clothes was a mistake. She started to turn to leave when a soothing voice was heard.

"Elise, please, join us." Garrett pulled out the chair next to him and offered it to her. She took it gratefully and placed her shaking hands in her lap. Garrett looked up at Stephen, who had not regained his seat. "Stephen, something wrong?" he asked.

This is really happening, he thought. The unknown servant girl was transformed into a glistening jewel. She certainly looked as if she could really be his sister in his mother's gown. He saw himself in her eyes, and therefore, his father. If only he had lived a few more months. If only he could have known his daughter, seen her like this, he would not have regretted what he thought was his biggest mistake.

This little sister was no mistake. He cleared his throat slightly and apologized. They took their seats, Stephen at the head of the table, with Elise and Garrett at his right.

The dinner passed slowly. Garrett was lost in thought, Stephen tried and failed to introduce topics of conversation, and Elise was overcome with unease. Several times, Garrett looked at Stephen sternly and tried to tell him with his eyes to ease up, but all Stephen could do was talk.

What would it have been like to have had a sister? He wondered. Someone to share duties and responsibilities with, someone to talk to about royal life. Things he couldn't talk to Garrett about. Things he hadn't allowed himself to say to his father.

"Do you like your room, Elise?"

A simple question, easy enough. "Yes….uh, thank you, um…." Answering proved to be more difficult than she expected with the large lump that was now in her throat.

"Splendid! And your journey here, was it pleasant?"

Garrett cleared his throat and tried to shake his head at his friend so he would stop.

Elise thought back to the carriage ride and days of traveling in fear and confusion. 'Pleasant' was not the word she would use, but she knew she must say something. "Uh….it was….alright?"

Stephen took enough from that to continue. "I enjoy traveling myself this time of year, so much sunshine and fresh air. Don't you?"

"Oh…" She began. "Well, I haven't done much…traveling."

"Yes, yes of course, well," Stephen was relentless. "Tell me about your home."

With this Garrett's eyebrows rose and he flashed an incredulous look toward the prince. Did he hear how ridiculous he sounded?

"My home…" She struggled to find words to questions she didn't want to answer, and felt more and more foolish with each vague reply. "Which one?"

Stephen laughed, thinking it was a joke, and tried to ease the awkward tension that had now formed among them. "Well, any of them, I suppose."

Eventually Garrett stopped trying to attempt to ease the battery of questions Stephen was throwing at this girl. Soon Elise could only respond with "yes" and "no", so little used to being expected to speak. She grew more overwhelmed with each question, and each attempt to answer.

Dishes were brought in and dishes were taken out, so many times that she lost count. Dainty appetizers and exotic foods each had a turn in front of her. She tried so hard to at least taste them, but the pit in her stomach churned with each small bite. If only he would stop asking her so many questions about a life she would rather forget. If only she was in a smaller room with normal food and a dress that did not belong to a queen.

No sooner did she think that when her unsteady hands dropped her glass, ruining the dress and turning her face bright red. Servants rushed to her aid from every angle, making her embarrassment worse.

"Oh, I am so very sorry!" she said as she tried to wipe the stains away. Her voice started to crack as hot tears of utter despair filled her eyes. Stephen attempted to put her mind at ease but she turned without pause and immediately ran out of the room, sobbing loudly.

He didn't know what to think. If this was what it was like to have a sister, it may be best not to tell her just yet.

Elise reached her room full of sobs. She barely made it to a basin before she lost every ounce of dinner she had managed to swallow. Tears flowed freely from the shame of how she had handled herself. Everything was wrong, the dinner, the dress, the questions, so many questions. How was she going to face them again? She pulled off the soaked gown and buried herself under blankets, letting the cool of the silk sheets comfort her hot, tear stained face. Maybe she would just stay in her room tomorrow.

"Well, that was encouraging" Stephen rolled his eyes in defeat.

"Maybe if you hadn't required so much conversation with her the whole time, she might not have been so intimidated!" Garrett had so rarely scolded him, Stephen wanted to laugh, but looking at his face he knew that he was serious.

"I'm sorry, I wasn't trying to be rude, and I was just trying to make her feel welcomed." Stephen defended himself.

Garrett checked his feelings for a moment before he continued to bash the prince. Well, might as well have done with it, now that he had started. "And I told you we shouldn't use the dining hall tonight. She doesn't need ten courses and grand style, she doesn't want to be impressed, she needs patience and time!"

Stephen knew he should just agree but he felt the need to state his reasons. "I just wanted to show her what she could have, if she chose this life. I wanted to show her what it meant to be a princess." He thought impressing her would help her to feel special. She was special. Finding out he had a sister, a piece of his father, it made her very special, indeed. The king loved lavish dinner parties for his guests, and he wanted to do what he thought his father would have done.

"If she chose?" Garrett was taken aback. So he did want to marry her. He was trying to win her. Why? He could have any woman he wanted. There was no shortage of eligible maidens for his choosing. Why was he trying so hard to impress this one? Tonight, he didn't care. He didn't want to know. He just wanted to grab one of his horses and ride away for a while, clear his head.

"Look Stephen, I don't know what's going on, and you certainly don't have to tell me. Let's just call it a night and we will figure it out in the morning." He let out a long sigh before adding, "And let's not have breakfast in the dining hall?"

He left to get a jacket from his room.

Stephen sat there, dumbfounded. It had been quite some time since he had such a conversation with his friend. What had him so riled up? Why was he so quick to take up for this girl?

Then all at once, it hit him.

A smile spread out over his face. It was suddenly clear that Garrett liked Elise, and he wondered if she liked him in return. Why, that would be perfect! They could marry and live in the Manor as Duke and Duchess. He could then confidently move into the castle. Garrett would not go away and Elise would be loved as his father wanted for the rest of her life.

Then he remembered how painfully shy she was. Perhaps wedding plans were too soon. He couldn't tell them about Elise being his sister yet. Garrett would think himself unfit for her and it would put too much pressure on Elise. Right now all she needed to focus on was being comfortable living in her new home. Well, that, and falling in love with the man he wanted to call his brother.

He sat back in his chair, delighted by this new distraction for his grief. He couldn't wait to watch this unfold. He took out some papers and started to make plans.

Hazel had knocked on the door softly before letting herself in. She had heard about the dinner party and knew Elise must be horrified. She called out into the dark room to see where Elise had hidden herself, and with nothing more than the glow of a weak fire she almost missed the head that peaked out from under the covers. Drawing her lantern closer she saw the tears covering her face and went immediately to her bedside to hold on to her. Elise gladly embraced the older woman and her sobs started all over again. Hazel just held her until it was over, gently petting the poor girls head. When the crying stopped, and the tears were spent, Hazel went to replenish the fire.

With the better lighting from the roaring fire, she helped Elise into her robe. She then sat her back down in front of the mirror and brushed her hair as she had done that afternoon. Looking into her own red, tired face was the last thing she wanted to do, but Hazel treating her with such pampering love was exactly what she needed.

"Now," Hazel said to her, "I want you to look in that mirror and tell me what you see."

For a moment Elise didn't know what to say. Then the anger at herself came to the surface and she whispered, "A failure."

"I thought you might say that." She put down the brush and sat next to her. "Let me tell you what I see. I see a beautiful young girl, who has seldom been shown kindness, never thought she was worthy of love, put into a situation that her life had in no way prepared her for. I see someone who is brave, in spite of her fears. Someone who is trying. Someone who will one day become the princess she was born to be."

Elise had to laugh at that last one. "I don't think 'distant cousin' is the same as 'born to be a princess."

Hazel only smiled. She knew Stephen hadn't told her, and whatever his reasons, she had to respect his wishes.

"Well then we shall just have to stop thinking of ourselves as 'distant cousin' then, Elise. However you are related, by whatever measure, you are still of royal descent. You have been brought here to overcome your past and rise to meet your future. I know you can do it, but you have to believe it, too."

"I don't know if I can do that" she said sadly.

When Garrett went into his room to get his jacket before going out to the stables, he realized that having Elise in the next room meant that he could hear everything she said. He didn't mean to eavesdrop, but hearing this exchange showed him so much more about this new princess.

"Poor girl" he whispered, and then he turned and went away.

On his way out the door with his head full of uncertainty and unspoken questions, he knew he needed the fresh air and sound of horse's hooves hitting the ground to center his thoughts. What did Stephen want from this girl? What did he want from him? Could he really stay here and watch two people who didn't even know each other to agree to that kind of marriage?

"Oh Garrett?" Stephen's voice was full of something Garrett hadn't heard often in the last year, merriment. "Since our new princess seems to be understood so much better by you, I'd like you to supervise her. Keep constant watch and teach her everything you can about your life here."

Garrett was shocked. First he goes to the end of the earth to find someone with some small measure of royal blood, making it clear that Stephen didn't consider him family, then he announces his intentions for her that take him even more out of the picture, and now he wants him to spend the last of his time here babysitting?

He gave him a hard look, said nothing, and then slammed the door on his way out.

Stephen was thrilled.

"This is going to work perfectly," he said to himself.

Minutes later, Garrett reached the stables, his mind racing with emotion. His horse, Raven, knew it was him and greeting him with excitement. "Hello, girl" he called to her. "Shall we go for a ride? Raven always helped him take his mind off his troubles and sort through things. Once the saddle was expertly fastened, Garrett led her out of the stables, mounted in one swift and confident movement, and took off into the woods.

His heart beat faster with each passing moment riding through the forest that separated the Manor from Westmore Village. Was the excursion making his heart beat so fast, or the events of the day? So much had happened already, he didn't know if he could take days like this every day. How would his time be spent now? Piano lessons and French? No, Stephen couldn't possibly ask him to teach her those things. He must mean for him to get her familiar with companionship so that she might know what their marriage would entail.

They rode for almost an hour. Raven seemed to respond to his every thought before he even knew what he wanted. Her slow walk became first a gentle trot, and then an invigorating gallop, seemingly knowing that Garrett needed the distraction. They trusted and respected each other completely. The wind in Garrett's hair made him feel like he was flying far away from his troubles. Out here, in the wilderness, he didn't have to answer to anyone, he was free to live by his own rules.

At the stables, coming back from his ride, Garrett thought he had a handle on things. So what if he had to babysit this girl? She was kind, beautiful, and since his friend desired some sort of business relationship with her, it wasn't betrayal if he enjoyed her company. Maybe he would even learn something. He could help her embrace companionship while he learned to embrace the loneliness that was sure to follow once the marriage had been made.

That's what his friend wanted, right? What other motive could there be for bringing her here? What other reason could he have for turning him into a chaperone, if not to separate himself from his companion, knowing the end of their friendship was near?

Just then, an eerie feeling crept over Garrett. He quickly turned and looked up at the Manor, as if he was being watched. His eyes met Elise, standing in her window. Was she watching him? He didn't know how to feel about that, only that he was drawn to her gaze. Looking like an angel standing above him, he wished he could hear her thoughts. She watched him intently as if lost in the moment, then catching his stare, quickly turned away and disappeared from view.

Chapter Four

The next morning, Elise was too embarrassed to join them for breakfast. This didn't surprise anyone. It was when she also stayed away for the rest of the day and onto the evening that they began to worry. Olivia announced that she had refused all offers of food.

"She will come around eventually." Stephen noticed his friend became more unsettled with each passing meal that Elise did not take part in.

"You might not be worried, but that doesn't mean there is nothing to worry about."

"Why don't you find out what this is about then, since it bothers you so much? You can't very well teach her companionship if she hides from you." Stephen found it difficult to pretend he was bored, when in truth he enjoyed the worry Elise's absence brought out in Garrett. He could almost hear wedding bells in the distance, his plan was working perfectly.

Garrett stormed down the halls on his way to her room. If this is how he was going to spend the rest of his short time, being pushed away by his best friend and preparing this girl to be his replacement, he might as well get started right now, without any further delay. He knocked loudly on her door, and when she didn't answer, his anger rose. Not caring about manners or politeness, he opened the door and all but stomped inside. What he saw took every bit of anger, resentment, and breath right out of him.

Elise was sitting on the floor, with her knees to her chest, crying. She was still wearing her night clothes and robe from the previous night, showing that she truly did refuse any type of care today. Her eyes were swollen slightly and her cheeks were red and hot. In between sobs she looked up at him, her expression was full of despair. Garrett was next to her in an instant, feeling so ashamed of his brief moment of anger. If his temper had caused her to crumble, he would never forgive himself. He wasn't even mad at her, he was upset about his situation; everything he was about to lose, and everything that had already slipped through his fingers.

"I'm sorry, I didn't mean to frighten you" he said softly, wishing he could hold her and wipe away her tears.

"What? You weren't, I mean, no you didn't scare me. I knew someone would end up looking for me, I just, I don't know" she said, before bursting into fresh tears. She was weak, shaking. Had this been going on all day? And it took this long for someone to check on her? Garrett was ashamed, he knew Stephen was pushing him away, but this girl really did need someone.

"Elise, I don't know what you are going through, but I'm here, and I'm not going to let you be alone like this again." He remembered comforting Stephen like this, in the final year of his father's life, several times. Stephen never showed his fears and sadness to his father, appearing so strong at all times, and Garrett was the only one who ever saw his pain. He would be here for Elise now, like he was there for Stephen. Especially since Stephen seemed suddenly eager to be rid of him.

"I'm just so afraid that I will wake up and be back where I was. After dinner last night I was sure someone would come and get me today and take me back there."

Garrett was saddened. Last night was supposed to be about welcoming her, and it did the opposite. Instead of making her feel at ease, it made her feel like a failure. They were putting way too much pressure on her. He looked around the room and noticed bedding strewn across the couch.

"Did you sleep at all last night?"

Elise dried her face and looked very confused. No one had ever wondered if she was ok, if she had slept. All she knew was fear. "I tried, but every time I closed my eyes, the nightmares started."

It took Garrett a few minutes to figure out what he should do. Elise sat, staring into the fire, sick with worry and fright. She had spent the whole night in fear of her past, and her whole day in fear of her future.

"Last night, at dinner, it was a mistake. But it was on our part, not yours. You see, Stephen wanted to give you a royal welcome, he's never been around people who didn't expect that from him. You in no way disappointed us, and we have no intention of sending you away," he thought of what she said about her dreams and added, "or forcing you to do anything you don't want to do."

"You aren't angry with me, or going to send me back?" Her tears had subsided, now it was only vulnerability. Garrett wanted so badly to hold her.

"I'm not angry, not at you, and you aren't going anywhere, unless you want to."

She smiled at him, and gently shook her head.

"Tell me what I can do to make you feel more comfortable." He helped her to her feet and led her to some chairs. She normally cringed when someone put their hands on her, but Garrett's touch was soothing. Besides, she was probably too weak from the ordeal of the day to make it herself.

Once she was seated, Garrett pulled another chair close for himself. He looked at her with compassion and kindly waited until she had collected her thoughts and was prepared to speak. She saw goodness in his eyes, something she felt she could depend on, trust even. Looking back at her life, Elise couldn't think of anyone else who had made her feel as safe.

"I'd like to know what is expected of me. I offered to work for my keep to Hazel, but she wouldn't let me."

Garrett tried to picture a princess in the kitchen, and laughed before becoming serious. "From what I understand, Prince Stephen is preparing to take the thrown. He will no longer need me, as a companion; but because you are all that is left in his bloodline, he wants you to marry him and become his permanent companion."

She was horrified, even though she had expected this. "Marry?" Perhaps her nightmares were not totally unfounded.

Garrett put his hands up to stop her fears, "Not a traditional marriage, by any means. He has made it clear that he sees this as a business relationship, because of your connection to the family."

She took this information in. If she had to marry him, but not in the traditional sense, it was still a better offer than any of the homes she had lived in previously. She would be bound yet again to a man who had expectations of her, but instead of violence, rage, and emptiness, she was being offered a life of luxury, ease, and friendship. "And how will I know what to do? How to behave?"

He looked uncomfortable, almost embarrassed. He paused to find the right words. "I've been put to the task of teaching you, before I go."

Elise looked worried. "You're leaving?"

Garrett hadn't said it out loud yet, he had to swallow the lump in his throat. "Unfortunately, yes. You see, kings don't have paid companions. I can't stay here, the royal family doesn't take on boarders. You either belong to the family, or you work for them." He had to stand up, walk away, do something to keep his eyes from watering. He rang the bell and asked the servant who appeared to bring Elise a dinner tray.

She saw a sadness in him that was both foreign and familiar. They were both facing an uncertain future. Garrett was afraid of going away from everything he ever knew, and she was afraid of going back to it. Wishing she could comfort him in the same way that he was doing for her, she tried to think of something to say. Maybe if he was distracted from the thoughts that haunted him, she could bring him a moment of peace.

"What is the prince like?"

He shrugged his shoulders and searched for the right words. "He's a good man. He will be a great king. Stephen is…."

What words could he use to build up his friend while he was angry with him? He had to put that aside for now.

"…kind. He is loyal, to his family; wise like his father with the people of the kingdom, but at the same time, gentle. I've never known him to be harsh. He takes his time and thinks things through. He wouldn't bring you here like this unless he had a plan for your future."

She felt her mind ease at these words. Kind, gentle, good? What a change that would be. "I am grateful for being brought here, and I did assume it was conditionally. But if it's only to be a friend to a good man, then I think I can learn to live with that. Are you certain that nothing more is expected of me? He won't send me back if I mess up again?"

"I think you have this all wrong, Elise." He must try to explain this to her, so she didn't get the wrong idea. "You are the one who is choosing. You don't have to accept him."

"What do you mean?" Choice was not something she was altogether familiar with.

"He is trying to impress you, so that you will see the life he is offering and accept him with it. That's what the big introduction and fancy dinner party was about." No wonder she was so nervous, if she thought she was the one who needed to impress them.

A new understanding came over her, a new perspective on this whole ordeal. She was being courted by this prince, pursued. All this time she thought she had to try to live up to his expectations, and all this time, he was just trying to make her feel welcome.

She looked up at Garrett and could tell he was ready to leave.

"Thank you, Garrett. I feel much better now. I shall have to face everyone tomorrow, but I will try to do what is asked of me."

He bowed his head, said goodnight, and retired to his room next door.

When her dinner arrived, she felt hungry enough to eat two. She was amazed at the amount of food that was brought, even more that she ate it all. Elise did not remember a time in her life of having so much to eat. She realized that her being here was a blessing. Now having something to do gave her a purpose, and she would apply herself wholeheartedly to it. She would learn to be a proper companion, and hope that marriage was a long way off.

Garrett went to his room and wept. Tears for the life he had led, the life he was going to teach someone else to have in his place. Where would he go? What would he do? All he knew was how to be a friend. He was too high in his field for service, but had no knowledge of anything more. Even Stephen seemed to be fading from him. All he had now was the girl who would take his place. All he had was Elise, and her silky brown hair, and her timid, clear blue eyes, and her soft skin.

Remembering himself, he stopped his thoughts. No, he couldn't allow himself to care about her, or become attached to her. He had to teach her, and then leave her.

It would hurt so much more if he loved her, as well.

Stephen sat quietly in his study, pondering the plans he was making. What if this didn't work? What if Elise wanted to leave because of his foolishness? What if he had no real reason for Garrett to stay? Then they would both leave, and he would be alone. He would rule a kingdom with no one at his side. The prince allowed himself a moment to picture that dark and dismal future, the only images coming to his mind were hollow and dim.

Shaking the images from his mind, he forced himself to stop. He had to try harder, find a way. He rang the bell and asked for Hazel, his housekeeper. She was the closest thing to a mother he had. She would know what to do. Less than five minutes passed before he heard her footsteps.

"You sent for me, sir?" Hazel needed little encouragement to come to his sofa and sit next to him. He had done this several times in the last year, seeking wisdom and comfort through his father's failing health. She was the one he spoke to about Elise the night he read that letter. He didn't tell her the full truth, but he suspected she knew.

"What am I doing wrong? I tried to do what my father would have done. I tried to show her such a welcome as he would have, and it seems to have caused so much trouble."

Hazel tilted her head and smiled at this man, who she still saw as a small boy. Someone who ran to her for bandages after scraped knees, or who promised to be good if he could have an extra sweet. The boy might have grown, but he would always be a child in her eyes. "You can't treat a poor country girl like a princess right away, my dear boy. Elise has been taken from a life of nothing but fear. She has been in houses with masters who have beaten her, starved her, and given her nothing but distain. It must be like living in prison. A dark, cold, frightful prison. Yes she is happy to be gone, but she is by no means free from it."

He thoughtfully shook his head. "What do you suggest?"

"Bring her out of her shell slowly, start very small. Treat her with nothing but kindness, and give her time. No more fancy dinner parties in the dining hall."

Stephen laughed. "That's what Garrett said."

Hazel cupped his cheek with her hand. "Such a smart young man he is."

An hour after Hazel left, there was a small, sheepish knock at his door. When he opened it, he found Elise waiting for him in a simple dress, not completely sure what to say. He was happy to see that she had at last left her room, but could tell by her pale complexion and tear stained face that she'd had a rough day.

"Elise, please come in," he stepped back and opened the door wider for her. She took a few slow steps into the room. "What can I do for you?" He was both surprised and elated to find her seeking him out so soon. He wished he could tell her he was her brother, but he knew she would need more time.

"I…wanted to come…and apologize…for…" She started.

He interrupted, "Please, the error was mine, entirely, I am the one who must ask forgiveness." He paused, wanting to change the subject to anything else. "Are you well this evening?"

"I am better now, thank you" How polite he was.

He offered her a seat and then sat behind his desk. She noticed a difference here, between the two men. Garrett sat very close to her when they were together, but Stephen kept his distance. She appreciated that from him, and wanted to learn more about him and start over.

Stephen looked cheerful as he began, now knowing how to proceed. "What can I do for you, while you are with us? This is your home now, for as long as you wish, and I want you to feel comfortable."

Elise smiled sheepishly and let out a short laugh of uncertainty. "I feel so out of place here. As though I might touch or break something or do something wrong." She looked up at his face and wondered if it was ok to tell him these things. "Not that I don't feel welcomed, you have been so gracious in opening your home to me. Where I come from, no one has even seen this part of the country, and here I am, living in it."

He smiled and shook his head, "Yes, I can imagine feeling out of place in a foreign land. I travel to several other countries surrounding us and I always feel strange at first. You get used to it after a few days."

There was a moment of silence now, both of them feeling very awkward.

"How often do you travel? Does Garrett go with you?" She wondered how much of her future marriage would be spend alone, or if she would be called on to attend these trips.

Prince Stephen shook his head. "Garrett prefers to stay behind. He often spends that time in the village with friends. I used to travel with my father, but now I suppose I will be going alone. Sometimes it's only for a few days, a week or so."

She was relieved that she wouldn't be asked to go with him. If the last few days showed her anything, it was that she wasn't ready for that kind of lifestyle.

Chapter Five

The next morning, the three awoke with a renewed energy. Stephen, trying to be patient, Garrett, determined to accept what he had to leave, and Elise, willing to embrace what she had been given. Breakfast was served in a very small room, only enough chairs for 6. Elise arrived first and quietly took a seat. She liked this much better, being the first in a room, having time to organize her thoughts. Garrett arrived next, a huge smile on his face seeing that she was present, and sat directly across from her. Stephen came in shortly after, taking the window seat. They were in a triangle, equal distances. A single server came in and presented a simple breakfast. Elise was relieved.

"I will be spending a few days at the castle" Stephen lied. He paused to see what effect this would have on them. Elise looked like she knew she should say something, but didn't know what. Garrett looked like he was waiting for him to continue before he formed an opinion. "I will be taking my place in the kingdom soon. There are a great number of details that I have to oversee at the castle before that can happen." He knew, of course, that he wasn't at all needed at the castle. His father had already settled everything for him, and Stephen could take control at any time. He thought that would seem like a more fitting place of refuge for a grieving prince than what he really had planned, getting away from everything to see Christina. He tried to ignore the pit in his stomach from telling such a bold faced lie.

"How long will you be gone?" Garrett seemed to be forming a plan in his mind.

"A few weeks, at least; more if necessary. You can send for me if anything happens that needs my attention, but I don't think that will be a problem. You two can handle things while I'm gone." Leaving the future permanent relatives in charge of Highfield Manor, having someone to come back to when he was done, knowing the two most important people in his life were so close by and safe? He liked how that felt. He could rule his kingdom knowing they were here. He couldn't say he knew Elise yet, but, she was his sister, of course that would happen in time. All that mattered today was that things were started to keep them both at the Manor. Together. The fact that he was lying, about his trip, about his reasons, about his own feelings, well that would have to wait.

Garrett showed almost no emotion. He knew this was meant to inform him that he had a job to do and that it needed to begin, so that it could end. He expected nothing more than this from Stephen now. If the prince wanted to push him away, he would not hold on. "See you when you get back."

Elise just stared at them both. Her future husband, or marital companion, or whatever he would be, was leaving her here? She hadn't spoken more than 10 sentences to him the whole time, knew almost nothing about him, and he wasn't going to stick around to learn anything about her. Maybe this is what she could expect, that she would stay behind while he leaves to tend to his duties. She certainly wouldn't mind that. She could live her life in quiet until needed, and perhaps that would be a seldom, brief amount of time. In that case, they didn't need to get to know each other much. Garrett seemed much more interesting anyways. She felt that she would really enjoy his company, even if it were only for a short time. He would tell her everything she needed to know about the prince in that time.

When breakfast was over, Elise took leave and bid Stephen goodbye. It was an awkward encounter, but she did it. Garrett nodded his head curtly at him and turned to leave, eager to be out of the room. "Garrett, just a moment please," Stephen motioned for him to join him, "you are free to use anything here that you need for Elise's teaching, any resource, whatever it takes." Stephen wanted him to use everything he could to please Elise. To make her want to stay, and to make her want to be with his friend.

Garrett didn't know what he should say. Companionship was taught to his 8 year old self in a matter of an afternoon. Basic manners and knowing he was to be a friend to the prince, not a servant, was all he needed to know. Why did Stephen want him impressing her? To make Stephen look good, he thought.

An hour later, Stephen had left and Garrett was in the parlor with Elise. "What would you like to do today?" He asked. If she was going to be a princess, she had to learn to make decisions.

She bit her bottom lip. "I don't know. What is it I am supposed to do?"

Garrett tried to think. "How about a tour of Highfield and the grounds? Then you can choose how you want to spend your time."

"Yes, thank you, I would like that." Her eyes brightened. That, she could do. She was certain she couldn't mess up a tour.

They spent the day strolling through each room, Elise tried to remember to ask questions, and Garrett answered them all graciously. They toured the library and he was pleased to discover that she read well. She told him about the tattered book she had brought with her.

"Before my mother died, she used to read it each night. It was only simple fairy stories, but I would fall asleep listening to her read them to me. All of our possessions were sold when she died, but they allowed me to keep the book, since it was already wearing down with use. They said it had no value, but it had more value to me then they could ever know."

"Did she teach you to read before she died?" He asked kindly.

Elise shook her head, "No, I was still too young then. One of the homes they placed me in when I was seven, there were two older children who already knew how, David and Martha. We used to play "governess" and I was often the student. Their parents worked all day so we had to take care of ourselves. Martha loved being in charge and giving us little assignments. David liked to teach "music" with pots and pans and I would teach "art" by drawing in the ground with sticks."

He smiled as he watched her tell the story. Her face was animated and full of life. It was like looking into a window of her soul. "How long were you able to stay with them?"

She sighed. "Almost a year, until their father was hurt and they couldn't afford to keep me any longer. They moved away after that. Thankfully no matter how often I was moved around, I could always keep my mother's book."

Her memories pleased him. How wonderful that she was able to keep something that had so much meaning to her, and her mother. "I lost my mother when I was 7, and I never knew my father. I spent a year with my uncle before the king asked for me. He was very happy to be rid of me."

"Garrett, that can't be true, he must have loved you, his own family."

"Oh no, my uncle loved the sea, and nothing else. He was fit to leave when my mother died and he had to take me in. He spent that time with me wishing he was on a boat. We were both happy when Stephens's father asked for me."

He invited her to select a few books for private reading, and had a servant put them in her room. Next they visited the portrait room. It was filled with paintings of all the royal members. Hundreds of years of family painted in the frames. Both of them silently wondered how Elise could be traced. Which portrait did she belong to? They came to the last two. King and Queen, Stephen's parents.

"They seem so familiar." Elise looked closely at the two.

"Stephen looks exactly like his father," Garrett observed. "When his portrait is painted, they will have a hard time telling which is which. You look like both of them, you know." Perhaps she was stolen as a baby, or her parents banished after some treacherous act. He wondered what branch of the family line she came from.

Elise looked at him. They seemed to share the same thought.

They went through several more rooms until it was time for dinner. They dined in a parlor that looked as though it had been seldom used, as both Garrett and the servants seemed to look about the room as if it was foreign. "Stephen wants you to use this room for your personal needs," he told her, "whatever you would like to use it for, it's yours. It will be kept at the ready at all times."

Elise didn't know what to say. They gave her a parlor? This whole, beautiful room, belonged to her? No room had ever belonged to her before. She had always shared a room with multiple children or slept in the servant's quarters. Just her bedroom here alone she counted as a luxury, but now a whole parlor?

Garrett took the opportunity to show her how to address the servants. He spoke to them with a mixture of respect and authority. At his polite requests, the room was arranged properly, the dinner was served and cleaned up, the fire tended to, and their every need was met. What's more, the manner in which he directed them made the servants happy to carry out his requests. He spoke to them as though he viewed them as equal, hardworking people, as they were. He must have had the same authority with them as Stephen had, since they were raised side by side.

Hazel came in, realized what Garrett was trying to do, and stepped up to help. As kind and loving to both boys as a mother, they both turned to her for guidance. As the head servant, who better to teach Elise how to address them? Garrett welcomed her help.

"Now Miss, this is our job, and we do it very well. I know you think that you should do everything for yourself, but then you are not allowing us to do our job. If you want to show us that you appreciate what we do, then please let us do it." She spent some time with Elise, directing the maids in the room, and encouraging her to do the same. It was very difficult for her. Even in her past life of service, she was not directed on what to do, or treated with any common decency. They threw her into a house and said to make herself useful, that was it.

No wonder she only lasted a year in each home before they kicked her out. Except for Mr. Devlin. He would have kept her forever. How long would she have been able to hold off his advances? How many nights would he have come home drunk, trying to get her in his bed? That last day, before the guards came, she saw such anger in his eyes; but she almost welcomed what could have been her last blow, it would have been better than what he wanted her to do.

Maybe that's why she wasn't afraid of the prospect of a celibate marriage.

The next day they toured the outer grounds. There were several acres of working fields, greenhouses full of flowers, decorative gardens for leisure. Dozens of workers were in the fields. "I had no idea the Manor had so many staff," Elise said.

"It doesn't. These fields are for the village. Anyone who spends a day working the field is allowed to take with them what they need for their family. It provides the people with quality food for honest work. My mother worked this field a few times to keep us fed, that's how I first met Stephen. He would play with the children who came with their families to work here.

Elise tried to picture Garrett as a boy. He was kind and gentle now, friendly, considerate, respectful. Is that why the King had chosen him? Was he like that as a child? It surely would have been a comfort for her, to have such a friend. He picked a bouquet from one of the greenhouses for her, and she accepted with a smile. The petals were soft and fragrant, the man that presented them to her was handsome and sweet.

They ended their adventure at the stables.

"Now this, this is my favorite place to be. Everything seems to fade, and I can just be myself."

Elise took in what she saw. She noticed a golden mare, a small black and white pony, an older grey horse, and a beautiful black stallion on one side, and on the other, a fleet of young white horses. Garrett anticipated her questioning gaze. "Those are the horses from the castle. Two for the carriage and the rest for the guards and messenger. They used to have only a small shelter here for the carriage horses, but Stephen had this built for me as a gift."

He led her past the horses until he came to the last, with that particular beauty he seemed to have a greater fondness. He spoke a soft greeting and the horse immediately came to him.

"This is Raven, one of my dearest friends." Garret gestured for her to come close, and when she approached the great horse, for the first time since he met her, she wasn't afraid. Garrett was confused. Elise suddenly appeared confidant, taking the horses reins and whispering softly, like she was talking to an old, dear friend.

"You have spent some time with horses before? Garrett offered.

Elise laughed at his surprise. "There is a small horse farm in my village, I used to visit when I could get a moment away from one of the homes I was placed in when I was younger. The stable hands let me spend time with them while my mistress slept each afternoon. She was elderly, a mean spirited woman, nothing I did was ever right in her eyes. I got through each day knowing I could visit the stables. I know exactly how you feel about them."

Elise had a glow about her while she spoke just now. Perhaps she had valued those horses as much as he valued his. The sun was beginning to set and its golden rays illuminated her glossy hair and added sparkle to her eyes.

He could look into those eyes forever, seeing the faint glow of life beginning to break free.

Elise felt his stare and didn't know what to say. She thought back through the events of the day, trying to think of something to say that would displace the awkwardness she felt. "Stephen seems to be a great man, from the things you have shown me these last few days. He cares about his home, and his people."

Garrett cleared his throat and turned around. Stephen. Right. Elise was meant for Stephen. Don't fall for her. Don't fall in love.

"I've kept you out too long today, it's getting late; we should go." Garrett spoke with as little feeling as possible, trying to drive out his emotions before they could take hold of his heart, before they could get deep enough to hurt him. He immediately walked out the door and waited to escort her back.

The sudden change in him was not lost on Elise. They walked back to the castle in awkward silence, Elise thinking she had done something wrong, and Garrett trying to stifle his feelings for her.

"I apologize if I was too familiar with your horse back there." She could only assume that was what caused his change.

Garrett looked confused. "Please, don't trouble yourself, I am out of sorts is all. You are welcome to visit the horses at your will, it would give me great pleasure. Goodnight."

He bowed slightly and quickly turned to leave. Elise just stood there for a moment, not knowing what to think, then she turned and walked slowly to her room, her mind racing with unease.

Garrett walked out to his balcony and leaned against the railing. He tried to clear his mind and make sense of what he was feeling. Now, more than ever, he could feel the heavy weight of his upcoming departure. For the first time in his life, he began to feel a sort of hatred toward Stephen. Looking out into the fields where he and Elise were just walking, he realized Stephen wasn't the only thing he didn't want to lose.

Brushing his fingers through his windswept hair, he caught sight of something glistening in the grass below.

"I wonder what that could be."

Turning for the door, he walked out of his room and went to retrieve it. It took some time to find it again, he almost decided to stop looking when he happened upon it. Reaching down to pick up the small, metal item, he saw that it was a necklace pendant of a silver dove.

"Elise must have dropped this." He said to himself.

He walked slowly back to the Manor, up the steps that led to their rooms, and knocked gently on her door.

"Who is it?" She asked, puzzled by the disturbance.

"It's just me, I think you dropped something, part of a necklace, maybe."

Suddenly the door jarred open and she quickly took the pendant from his outstretched hand. "I can't believe I was so careless. Thank you, Garrett, you have no idea what this means to me."

He smiled, pleased to see he had brought her joy. "I saw it from the balcony, you should really get a chain for it so it doesn't fall down again."

"I hope to, some day. It's silly, but I used to hold it and think of myself as that little dove, flying swiftly in the wind. I told myself that someday, when I was free to live my own life, I would have it as a proper necklace, and wear it every day."

She looked up at him, her eyes bright and cheerful, and it made his heart dance.

"I hope you get to wear it, someday soon."

Chapter Six

As they were finishing with breakfast the following morning, Elise wondered what they would be doing that day. Garrett was quiet, and seemed to have much on his mind, so she sat and waited patiently for him to gather his thoughts. He put his teacup down and addressed her.

"We are having visitors today." Garrett spoke carefully, not wanting to frighten her with his plans.

She looked confused and unsure of what to say to him. "W-we? Visitors?"

Taking her hand gently, he began to reassure her. "Well, sort of." He smiled. "You see, I am having visitors. Every few months some very good friends of mine come visit me for the day from the village. I've known Jane all my life, and her husband Henry is our town apothecary. I think it would be a wonderful opportunity for you to get to know some of the people here, and I would be pleased if you would join us."

Elise pondered this information. It sounded as though she had a choice to make. He wasn't telling her, he was asking her. Garrett was so kind and considerate, surely his friends would be as well. "Thank you, I would like that very much."

"Excellent" He said as he rose from the table. "I must speak with Hazel before they arrive, if you would excuse me."

She gave him a smile and a nod. He bowed slightly before going out of the room.

Once he was gone, Elise was alone in the room. Her hands began to shake so she grasped them together. "What if I say the wrong thing?" She wondered. "What if they don't like me?" As the old fears began to take hold of her mind, she remembered what Garrett had told her. She wasn't there to impress anyone. So why was she so nervous about meeting these people?

Because they were Garrett's friends. She wanted his friends to like her. Maybe she even wanted Garrett to like her. She sighed deeply and put her hands on her forehead. "What are you getting yourself into?"

She walked to her room and Olivia helped her change out of her morning dress.

"Do you know the people who are coming here today, Olivia?"

The maid was quick to reply. "Oh, yes, of course. Jane and Henry are the very best of people, you know."

Elise pressed for more information, thinking it would help settle her nerves. "Garrett said they come here often, what do they do during their visits?"

Olivia finished securing her dress and moved on to freshen up her hair. "Just talk is all, like friends do."

She didn't have much experience with those. Elise hoped she would know what to say and that they were kind.

When she was dressed for her company she opened her door and stepped out. Garrett was just about to walk into his room when she stepped out of hers.

"Hello" he said to her with a smile. "Almost ready?"

She smoothed her hands over the dress and sighed. "I suppose."

"You'll do fine." He smiled. Who wouldn't love her? "I just have to grab something first."

He retrieved an item from his room and slipped it into his pocket on his way out. She saw it was a small, wooden item. He offered Elise his arm and she willingly took it, and they walked together into the hall to wait for his friends. Garrett was beaming, like he had a secret. He heard the carriage arrive at the door and he turned to Elise, his eyes shining with anticipation. "They're here."

Elise realized she was holding her breath and forced herself to relax. The door opened and her eyes softened when two little blonde heads came into the room. Garrett didn't tell her they had children!

They screamed in delight and ran to Garrett. He released her arm and held his out to them in welcome. Both children hugged him tight, almost knocking over the strong man. "Uncle Garrett!" the boy shouted. "Have you made another horse for us?"

Garrett laughed and returned to his feet, the little boy stood back in anticipation while his sister held on to Garrett's hand. He used his free hand to reach into his pocket. "Another horse?" He asked playfully. "I've made you nearly a dozen! You couldn't possibly want more?"

The little girl twirled around and hugged him tight. "We always want more horses Uncle Garrett! I know you made one for us!"

Then, taking his hand out of his pocket, he presented a beautifully made wooden horse. The children gasped in delight at the new toy and instantly went to grab it, but he closed his hand over the treasure. "Now I know," he said quietly, "that your parents would like to see you use your manners before running off to play." He nodded his head toward Elise, who was charmed by their display of open affection. The children looked at her and immediately stiffened, knowing he wouldn't release the toy until they had politely introduced themselves.

Elise, please allow me to present Alexander and Amelia, the twins.

Little Alexander bowed while his sister curtsied. "Pleased to meet you, ma'am."

She was delighted. Children put her at ease in an instant, and she felt some of her insecurities vanish. She thanked them both graciously.

Amelia whispered something into her brother's ear and he was quick to action. "Now may we have the horse, Uncle Garrett?"

He placed the figure into Amelia's hand. "Of course you may! Now run along and try not to get into too much trouble." He winked at them as they giggled and ran off.

"Charming little ones, how old are they?" Elise asked.

"I'm supposed to say six and a half, as they like to say. It's no longer dignified in their eyes to be only six." He laughed.

The door opened again and the adults approached. A couple came in, a little older than Garrett, but with kind faces. They had dusty blonde hair, darker than their children. Garrett introduced his friends and Elise was warmly accepted. Hazel announced that tea had been served for them in the main parlor. Garrett took the lead and again offered Elise his arm. She accepted it at once and Jane gave her husband a knowing look. Henry smiled and nodded at her, understanding her instantly and agreeing.

Once they had sat down to enjoy their tea, Jane was the first to speak. "Elise, Garrett tells us that you are not from this part of the country, have you enjoyed your stay so far?"

Elise thanked her for her question, "Yes, quite. Garrett has made me feel…." Her eyes met his gaze and she blushed softly before turning away. "…very comfortable here."

Jane's eyebrows raised at her friend as she answered. "I see, I'm sure he has." She cleared her throat in the direction of her husband and Henry was quick to jump in.

"How much of the town have you seen, my dear? Have you been to the village or the castle?"

Elise wasn't sure what to say. She hadn't been anywhere besides the Manor, and that was fine with her. "Well, I…"

After a moment of hesitation Garrett came to her rescue. "Not quite yet, Henry, I didn't want to overwhelm her."

Henry chose a delicate sandwich from the tray and nodded his approval. "Probably best."

Jane liked Elise immediately. After tea, she sat next to her on the sofa for a more intimate conversation while the gentlemen busied themselves with talk about the village. She told her about her children, her husband's work, and the life they had built. Elise learned that Jane was a midwife, and was instantly filled with questions.

"I'm sure you must have so many stories." She asked in wonder. Elise had always been drawn to children, babies especially. Having helped deliver a few herself in her own past made her understand her friend's stories better than anyone else.

Jane stirred a sugar cube into her tea and smiled. "Oh yes, countless stories. I've been a midwife here for five years, after apprenticing my aunt before she passed."

"I have been fortunate enough to witness a few births in my time of service, nothing like you have seen, I'm sure." Elise sheepishly confessed.

Jane put her cup down and leaned forward in excitement. "Have you now? That is something! Tell me about them, please."

Elise felt a bit uncomfortable, surely this accomplished midwife would think her limited experiences were dull in comparison. "Oh, well, let me see." She thought back to the times in her past when she was part of such events.

"When I was around twelve, I remember our home was next to the home of an older, childless couple. The husband knocked at our door one night, he was frantic with worry for his wife. The doctor was there but he had told the man to find a servant, because he needed help. I was sent, thinking perhaps he needed more bandages or supplies, but when I got there, I couldn't believe what I was seeing." She paused briefly to glance around the room, then lowered her voice.

"The woman was in bed, holding her stomach, and the doctor was trying to explain that she was having a baby."

Jane's eyes grew wide. "She didn't know??"

Shaking her head, Elise continued, "No, the poor woman had waited so long to have a child, she thought her time had passed. The doctor told me to run for the midwife, but by the time I had found her and we had gotten back, the baby was already born. She had me sit and hold the baby to keep it warm while she attended to the mother."

"It's really something, isn't it?" Jane spoke lovingly. "Holding a newborn baby?"

Elise smiled sweetly at the memory. "Oh, yes, it was magical. Does it ever stop feeling like that?"

"No, that I can assure you. Every time it feels just like that." Jane nodded. "You said there was another birth?"

Elise felt so comfortable talking to her new friend. She never had someone she could share things like this with.

"Yes, one of my favorite homes, a young couple, Grace and Frank, were expecting a new baby, and I was placed with them to help care for him when her time came. Grace was very kind to me, and asked me to help her when it was time for the baby to come. She and I became very good friends. I remember when it was time, the midwife explained many things to us. She said the baby would take a long time to arrive, but that it was normal for the first."

Jane nodded, "Yes, that's usually the case. Tell me, what happened with this couple, are they still in the town?"

Elise shook her head. "No, a few months after the baby was born, they moved. I don't know where. Hopefully somewhere nice for their children to grow up." She had a tone of sadness in her voice. She had missed her friend terribly, but knew that getting out of the poor country town was better for their family.

Olivia came in to refresh their tea tray, and Elise realized she had been doing most of the talking.

"How do you know Garrett?" Elise asked, redirecting the conversation back to her friend.

Jane looked back at him and smiled, then turned to Elise. "His uncle's house was two houses down from mine. When Garrett lived with him, we would run off and play behind our houses. I have only brothers so I was more accustomed to playing pirates and having races than playing dolls and dress up." She laughed as she remembered their past. "We would get into so many scrapes! Climbing trees and exploring the forest. I was a bit older than him, but ah, the fun we had!"

Elise could imagine him as a passionate and willful child. Watching him with Jane's children, she pictured how he would be with his own.

"You're good for him, you know" Jane smiled knowingly at her new friend. "I think he has taken a liking to you, as well."

Elise blushed heavily at the words. "I don't know what you mean…."

Jane took her hand gently. "And I believe you may feel something toward my friend?"

She looked at her in shock. How did she know?

Just then, the children came into the room, and rushed over to their mother. Amelia was crying about her brother for breaking the precious toy when Alexander came quickly in to defend himself. After determining it was an accident and Garrett promising to make another to replace it, he proposed a plan.

"It's alright, children, I have just the thing to make you both feel better." He glanced at Jane and Henry, who nodded their approval. "Why don't we go out to the stables and see the real horses?"

Their cries turned to sheer joy at the prospect of a new adventure. All six of them walked out to the stables, enjoying the fresh air and marveling at the season. As they approached the horses, Garrett spoke to Jones, the stable hand, and asked for the black and white pony "Blithe" to be brought out. He explained to the children that they could each have a turn riding with him around the fence.

Elise's heart grew even softer as she watched how kind and careful he was with each child, making the simple ride an adventure for them. Her own experience with horses made her feel closer to Garrett in this moment. She caught his eye and they smiled at each other, feeling the warmth from the sun, the freshness in the air, and the thrill of the activity.

After dinner the children fell asleep, and Henry mentioned to his wife that they needed to be getting home. Jane hugged Elise tight and whispered in her ear, "I'm always here for you if you need to talk."

Elise thanked her sincerely, shook Henry's hand, and waved goodbye as they carried their sleeping children to the carriage. As the door closed behind them, Garrett turned toward her. "Did you like them?"

She nodded and smiled at him, "Oh, very much, thank you for letting me meet them."

He took a step closer to her. "Of course."

Elise could feel her heart beating fast with every passing moment. His passionate eyes went all the way to her soul, and he looked very much like he was going to come closer, when suddenly they heard the carriage pull back up to the front. The couple turned their heads, expecting to see Henry coming to claim a forgotten item, when Stephen walked in.

"Good evening!" He said to them both.

Elise looked up at Garrett. She was blushing, while Garrett's face had gone pale. He instantly took a step back from her, put his hands behind his back as if he had been caught stealing something, then turned and walked away.

Stephen looked suspicious. "Am I…interrupting something?"

Elise snapped back into reality, shook her head, and turned to the prince. "No Stephen, we were just….saying goodnight." She stumbled around for something to say, anything. "How was your trip?"

He walked over to his office and gestured for her to follow, happy to have someone to greet him on his arrival. "Everything went very well, thank you. I saw the apothecary's carriage and thought someone was ill, but the footman assured me they were here for a visit."

She was relieved that Stephen wasn't going to talk about what he almost saw in the hallway. Elise didn't even know what it was she would have been covering for. Maybe she imagined it, the spark she felt between them.

"Yes, we had a lovely time, and Garrett has been…."

She hesitated, suddenly not knowing how to finish the sentence. Garrett had been what? Charming? Confusing? Dashing? She could say any number of things to describe the last two weeks. Stephen noticed her pause and looked up from his desk, his eyebrow raised in anticipation.

"A perfect gentleman."

His brow softened as she said this and he sat down. "Good, very good."

He spent a few minutes talking to her about his trip, still maintaining the vise of being at the castle. While his feelings for Catherine were blossoming at a fast pace, he still felt that it was not the right time to make those feelings known to his friend or sister. He didn't want his own romance to take precedence over theirs, if there was one. Elise stayed and spoke with him for another half hour, and then said goodnight.

Stephan was pleased with how easy it was to talk to her this time. She wasn't feeble or scared like she was before he left. What a difference these weeks had already made in her confidence level. He felt that she would make a fine ruler someday.

Over the next few days, Stephan and Elise got to know each other better. They would often be found in his office, or in a sitting room, always with something in between them; a desk, a sofa, a fireplace. He seemed to want to be in the room with her, but not close to her like Garrett. She asked him questions about his life and the things he liked. Stephan found her curiosity encouraging, thinking she was enthusiastic about her future life as a royal. In reality, she was sizing up his expectations of her once they were married. She still wasn't thrilled with the idea, but compared to the life she had waiting for her back home, the prospects of being safe and secure seemed like the obvious choice.

During this time, Garrett kept his distance. He seemed to have lost the openness and spirit he had previously shared with Elise. He was present in the house, but his mind was far away. Every time Stephen came into the room and tried to start a conversation, he would find a reason to leave. If the prince only knew the pain and agony he was causing his friend and how he was misunderstanding the situation, he would surely have told him the truth.

Garrett was summoned to the prince's room one evening, and he found Stephan walking about the room with his manservant. He immediately noticed trunks open on the floor and assumed he was leaving again.

"Please don't tell me it's a honeymoon trip" he thought to himself, bracing for the words he was dreading. He wasn't ready to leave his home yet, wasn't ready to leave Elise. He cleared his throat and then leaned on the doorframe with his arms crossed over his chest.

Stephen looked up. "Ah, there you are. I'm planning on another long visit to the castle, leaving tonight actually."

It certainly was easier when he was gone, but Garrett felt like picking a fight. "Again? Didn't you just come back from there?"

Stephen looked away and pretended to busy himself with his arrangements, hoping his friend didn't see right through his lie. "Yes, well....I have a few more things to take care of."

Garrett rolled his eyes and let out a distrustful sigh. Of course he knew his friend was lying, about this trip and the previous. He never made long trips to the castle before, usually he would go and be back within a day. Making wedding plans, more likely. He never hated someone so much.

"So what do you need me for?" He was ready to get this over with.

The indignant tone was not lost on Stephen. This kind of attitude was exactly why he wanted to go see Christina again, she was far better company.

"I just wanted to make sure you could handle things while I'm gone, and that you were getting along well enough with Elise. I need to know I can count on...."

Garrett straitened up and uncrossed his arms, his hands forming fists out of anger. He interrupted the prince, "Count on me??" His eyes were fierce. "You think I haven't been taking care of her? That I can't take care of her?!"

"Garrett come on, I didn't say that, I didn't mean…" He looked at the angered face of his best friend and felt like they were slipping apart in a way that couldn't be repaired. He sighed and looked at him, not knowing what he could say that wouldn't just make things worse. He didn't have to think about it very long, as Garrett shot him an ominous look, turned around, and left.

Time. Garrett just needed more time. Maybe he would extend his visit with Christina's family another week.

Garrett walked to his room and shut the door, hard. He plopped down on his bed and threw the pillow across the room. "The nerve of that guy," he thought to himself, "thinking I couldn't take care of her." No sooner had he thought the words when they came right back to him. The anger drained from his face and turned into panic. "Well, maybe he's right." He turned in his bed to face the wall, hiding himself. He knew he could provide a loving, stable home. He had enough for them to both live quite comfortably, but it was nothing compared to the life Stephen could give her. Choosing between a life with him or the crown, the choice was painfully obvious.

Chapter Seven

The next day, Elise was to be fitted for new clothes. A dressmaker from Westmore and her assistant took over one of the front rooms. A large dressing screen was arranged so that Elise could have privacy, which made it acceptable for Garrett to come in and help her choose different styles. He had put away all of the sadness he had felt the previous night, and had resolved to enjoy what time he had left. Elise was so overwhelmed by all the choices and he tried to help as best he could.

The dressmaker held up a light green print and Elise turned her eyes to Garrett for his approval. He easily read the look of disappointment in her eyes. "No, that's not right for her. Try the other one."

Next a lilac color was shown and she glowed under the fabric. "That one's good" he truthfully spoke.

She smiled at him and spoke softly. "I like this one, too."

The dressmaker wrote down colors and measurements in her book and then excused herself while she consulted with her assistant. Garret stood up and walked about the room, playing with fabric samples, tossing them aside and snatching the ones that caught his eye. He threw one at Elise and she was slightly taken aback, before she noticed the playfulness in his smile.

"Watch out!" She laughed "Or I will stab you with one of these dress pins!"

Garrett smiled. "Oh really, princess?" he picked up a bolt of fabric and held it in front of him like a mighty shield. "I would like to see you try!"

She shook her head at him. "I don't know how I'm going to get through the rest of this, it's so hard to know what to choose!"

Garrett put the fabric down and walked up to her. "It's easy. Just tell them what you want."

She looked at her reflection in the mirror. "Just like that? Easy for you to say. You already know how you are supposed to look and what you are supposed to want."

"Elise, it doesn't matter what you are supposed to want. Figure out what it is you truly want, and you can't go wrong. You want the blue one? Pick the blue one. You want this ugly yellow one, pick the ugly yellow one. You can have anything that you want."

She turned towards him and looked him up and down. "Anything?" She asked, not intending for that to sound quite so flirtatious, even though she meant it.

"Well, uh…um…" He cleared his throat and let out an uncertain chuckle while running his hand through his thick hair.

Was he blushing?

"H..here, just pick this one…" He stammered and he picked up the blue fabric, tossing it at the table before returning, flustered, to his seat.

Elise giggled at his awkwardness and went behind one of the screens. She was just teasing, but a part of her did know exactly what she wanted, and it had nothing to do with dress colors. Did she really have that much of an effect on him? She wondered.

"Alright then, bring me the blue one and I will see if I want it." Her cheeks began to glow in anticipation as she walked behind the screen.

Garrett got up, shook his head at himself, and picked up the fabric bolt. He tried to hand it to her from the other side of the screen but she asked him to bring it closer. He walked over and handed it to her without showing any emotion at all, but Elise was beginning to see through him. She draped the fabric over her shoulders and then called his attention.

"Well," she asked, her breath catching in her throat, "do you like it?"

Garrett's mood softened as he looked at her, draped in the deep blue fabric. It brought out the blue in her eyes. He could get lost in her eyes. He swallowed and his breathing became shallow as he answered in a deep, wanting voice. "Yes."

Her eyes searched his as her heart began to pound. He took a step closer to her, close enough to whisper.

"Do you like it?" He asked about the fabric, but neither of them were talking about dresses now.

She reached up and touched his rugged cheek with her hand. He shifted his feet and she turned into his embrace. "Very much" she whispered. She could feel his heart beating through his chest as he looked from her eyes to her soft lips. His hands slipped around her waist and pulled her closer. He whispered her name as if it was a question, and she knew he was asking for permission.

That's when the dressmaker came back in and called for her.

Their eyes went back into focus as they realized what almost happened. Garrett's eyes were now full of fear while Elise just stood in confusion. They both turned away quickly. Garrett wished them well and excused himself.

Each of the following mornings, they had breakfast in Elise's parlor. They began looking the part of Master and Mistress of the house. Garrett told her it would be her responsibility to instruct the servants while they were there, and she very meekly made her requests known to them. She knew he was trying to get her used to it, and she was grateful for the practice before Stephen came back to see her progress.

Garrett watched her silently. The last month showed him many more skills she already possessed. She could read, write, draw, enjoy art, had easy, pleasant manners, and seemed to be comfortable with horses. Maybe he could get her to ride one.

"I'd like to go into the village today, Elise. Would you accompany me?"

She smiled. "Of course, it would be my pleasure." How easy it was to say yes to him now.

They finished breakfast and she dismissed her servants. Garrett left to arrange the carriage and Elise went to her room to change into a traveling dress. She asked Olivia in to help her.

"How far away is the village, Olivia?" Elise asked as she was helped into the gown.

"I'd say half an hour's ride, Garrett likes to go through the woods, it is beautiful this time of year. "

Elise felt a sense of adventure rising in her very soul. She felt she could go anywhere with Garrett, but a carriage ride through the woods with only a few attendants sounded romantic and thrilling. She would have to focus on thrilling instead of romantic. At least there would be a few servants with them. She finished dressing and opened her door to find Garrett waiting quietly for her. When he looked up at her, his eyes shone with delight as he held out his arm for her to take. "Are you ready?" His words sent a chill over her shoulders. Oh yes, she was ready. For whatever awaited her, as long as she was with him.

As they stepped outside, Elise stopped abruptly. Expecting to see a carriage and attendants, she saw a single groom holding the reins of two horses, Raven and the golden mare. Garrett looked at her with questioning eyes, eyes that held hope and promises, and she knew she would be safe with him. "I was expecting a carriage," she said with a laugh, "but I can see you have other plans?"

He gently squeezed her hand, still wrapped tightly around his arm. "I don't think a carriage would fit where we are going." He winked and smiled at her, and she felt her cheeks warm.

Garrett helped her onto her horse gently and began to give her instruction. Elise held back laughter. She knew very well how to ride a horse from her time at the stables, but she liked the idea of having a skill Garrett didn't know about yet. She enjoyed his attentions and decided to play along for a while.

Once they were both on their horses, he led them out slowly beyond the Manor gate, into a stretch of woods several miles wide. These woods separated Highfield Manor from

Westmore village. They followed a smooth path that was lined with large trees. The leaves moved softly in the late summer breeze that kept them cool. Birds flew up above them, singing their morning songs. Garrett led the way, taking care to go slowly, keeping her horse close behind as to guide her through the woods. Suddenly, Elise knew she could contain herself no longer. She moved from a side saddle position by swinging her leg over to the other side of the horse, and knowingly commanded the magnificent beast to do her will. Within moments, she was galloping past Garrett, laughing and bidding him to keep up if he could.

It took him only a moment for his mind to go from confusion to elation. He beckoned his horse to go faster and faster until he caught up to Elise. She looked as if she belonged here. She was fearless and free, commanding the horse as though she had done so all of her life. Her hair blew wild and her cheeks flushed with life. Garrett had to work hard to keep up with her, finally resolving to use a shortcut he knew well. When he bounded out on the path in front of her, she stopped her horse to catch her breath, smiling brightly. He looked at her with a mixture of delight, mock vexation, and a desire to know this woman even more. Raising an eyebrow at her with an air of pretend scorn, he spoke, "I see I underestimated you, Princess. You could have told me you could ride like this when we started."

Elise laughed at his mockery, "I would not have missed the opportunity to surprise you! You were so intent on teaching me, I didn't have the heart to stop you."

Garrett reached up to a low branch, plucked a leaf, and tossed at her. "Ah, but you were more than happy to make a fool out of me, I see I shall have to watch out for you."

He was close enough now that if she reached out her arms, she could touch him. "Are you afraid of me, Garrett?" Her eyes danced with merriment.

The question was in jest, but it caught him off guard. He was afraid, of wanting something he couldn't have, of leaving the only home he knew, and of losing himself in the gaze of the angel in front of him.

Elise was confused as she watched his face take on a sad, pained expression. He suddenly looked so lonely, so fearful. She started to reach out to him when he roused himself, smiled, and turned his horse around. "We are here, let's continue."

He rode beside her now, and they entered the village together. They rode slowly as Garrett pointed out his father's old home, houses of friends, and things he liked about the quaint little town. Everyone they passed waved at him and smiled at her, wondering who she was. There was even a few glares of jealousy from some of the prettiest girls, and Elise enjoyed the assumption that Garrett was hers.

Soon they came upon the home of the messenger. Garrett said he had some business there, and asked Elise to wait for him. He dismounted from the horse and was impressed when she did the same, without help. She told him she would walk around to the shops and he could catch up when his business was finished. He nodded, retrieved a folded piece of paper from the inside pocket of his jacket, sighed deeply, and walked inside.

Elise strolled over to the center of the town, where a large well stood. She pulled the bucket out and took a drink with the ladle. As the cool water quenched her thirst, she wondered what business Garrett was attending to. If he needed a message sent, why not use the royal messenger? And why did he look so dejected as he entered the building?

She put the ladle back and lowered the bucket into the well. Scanning the village, she noticed a flower shop and walked towards it. As she entered through its doors, the heavenly aroma of fresh and inviting flowers intoxicated her. She closed her eyes and breathed deeply, marveling at the heavy, perfume like scent. Opening her eyes, her gaze focused. The clerk greeted her and offered to show her the many flowers on display. Elise was puzzled with his formal greeting and then realized how she must look. She was wearing one of her newly made dresses, her hair, though it had come down from its previous style during the ride, now laid on her shoulders in soft, flowing curls. She must look like a refined lady to him. How would he have greeted her if she had opened the door dressed in the rags she was wearing on that first day? With tangled hair and tear stained cheeks? Now that she dressed the part, she must learn how to act the part as well.

She gave the clerk a small curtsy and asked a few simple questions. He answered them all with abundance, thrilled with the prospect of entertaining a lady. He did his best to cater to her feminine charms and pointed out the prettiest, and priciest flowers. Elise was flattered by such attention and was happily amused as she waited for her escort.

Garrett found difficulty in addressing his request to the town messenger, a man named Tom. "Well now, this is an odd request from you. If I had royal messengers at my disposal, I would use them. They would get you an answer much faster." Tom said from behind his spectacles.

"I am not in a hurry, and I'd like as few people to know about this as possible." Garrett answered with determination.

"I don't see a problem with that," the man said, "I'll get this sent out to the towns you specified." He noticed Garrett's sad expression. "Don't worry so much, son. People move sometimes, it won't cause a scandal. Unless of course," he lowered his voice and leaned in closer, "you don't plan to go alone."

He gestured to Elise at the well. He must think they were running away together. What a pleasant idea. For a fleeting moment he thought of the look on Stephen's face upon finding them gone away together. He smiled mischievously and then shook his head. "No sir, just trying to slip away gracefully."

Tom nodded and said, "All right, check back in a few weeks and we should hear something by then".

Garrett stepped out into the warm sunshine. He walked slowly to the well and took a drink, as Elise had. The cool water quenched his thirst, but did nothing for his breaking heart. He looked about the village and thought back on his life. He loved it here. Yes he was put into service, but in the best possible way. He had a life here, a good life, he was happy and thriving. He knew he could take a house in the village, he was paid handsomely by the palace and had saved most of it. Never having to spend any of the money, the royal family supplied all of his needs. But then he would be only miles away from his best friend who no longer wanted him and the woman he couldn't have. He knew the day was coming that he would have to leave.

"Hello, dear" a friendly voice spoke next to him, bringing him out of his lonely thoughts. "Come to visit me now?"

"Jane," he said kindly to his friend. "I thought I might run into you, I have a gift for the twins." He pulled a box out from the horse's satchel. Jane opened it to find half a dozen horse figures.

"Oh Garrett, how lovely! They are beautiful, but, why not wait to give these to them yourself?"

He smiled but had a pained expression. "I just wanted to make sure they got to them. I don't know how much longer I will be here, so I made extra."

She looked at him, worried and confused for her friend. "What's going on?" Jane sat down at the well and invited him to sit next to her, which he did without hesitation. "Please, you know you can tell me anything."

Garrett let out a long sign, and turned to face her. "Everything is being torn apart and taken away from me. My time at the Manor is drawing to a close, and I will soon be without a place to call home, or people to call friend."

"You know you will always be welcome in this village, you need not fear your future" Jane said calmly.

"But I won't have a home here, nor anywhere close to here. I couldn't live so close to the Manor or the Castle, knowing I wasn't welcome there anymore."

Jane thought for a moment before she replied. "I've known you, and Stephen, for a long time. I've never seen truer friends. I understand you may not be needed, but I know for a fact, you are wanted."

"I had thought the same, for a long time. Now," Garrett shook his head softly, "I'm not so sure."

"Were will you go?" Jane asked.

"I don't know yet."

"Well," she smiled, "when you do go, just take that pretty girl with you, and you'll never be lonely a day in your life."

Garrett looked up at her, shocked. She winked at him and his shock turned into a smile, his eyes danced, and his cheeks colored.

Jane got up to leave, "She's in the flower shop, by the way." She looked sideways at him and gave a slight chuckle. Suddenly, she turned her head to the sound of her children beckoning to her. She gave a nod to Garrett and went to join them. Once she was gone, Garrett allowed himself a brief moment to ponder. What if he really did it? What if Stephen came back to an empty house? He could run off into the sunset with her. He wondered, would she go with him if he asked? What's more, would he forgive himself for denying her the crown?

Shaking the fantasy from his mind, he knew the answer to the last question, but he wasn't ready to let go of the dream.

Garrett opened up the door to the flower shop and found Elise sitting in a chair, surrounded by two or three men, hanging on her every word. She seemed to be enjoying this new attention, and accepted it graciously. She was doing her best to talk to them. He could tell she was nervous, she bit her bottom lip whenever she felt like that. Seeing him approach, her eyes lit up. She jumped out of her chair and came up to him with a look of admiration in her eyes. "Well

Jane, wouldn't I love to follow that advice?" he thought to himself.

"There you are!" she said as she approached him, curling her hand around his arm in a way that let the men in the shop know she was not available. "Where to next?"

Her sense of adventure and complete trust in where he would take her made him ache for the future they could have together. He wanted to know her more, see where she would lead him. "Where would you like to go?"

She considered this for a moment. "Let's take a walk and find out." She took his hand and led him out of the flower shop, while Garrett smiled at this new direction and felt the willingness in his soul to follow her.

They walked along the town center slowly, hand in hand. Garrett didn't care where she would take them, as long as she was with him. She spoke about the differences between Westmore and her own small town, and seemed to like it here so much more. He felt at home here with her. Suddenly they paused, hearing someone call out from behind.

"Elise? Is that you?"

They both stopped, perplexed that someone here would recognize her. A wave of fear passed over her, thinking it was someone looking to take her back to Mr. Devlin. Garrett seemed to share her thoughts, he gave her a calming look; then slightly nodded his head to her, letting her know that he would keep that from happening. She turned into the direction she was called and saw a face from her past, but this was the one face in the world that she was happy to see again.

"Grace?"

A woman a few years older than her came rushing over to them. Elise let go of Garrett's hand and threw her arms out to welcome her friend. "I can't believe it's you! It's been such a long time!"

Grace had tears of joy in her eyes. "I thought I would never see you again!"

Garrett stood silently watching the ladies. How did she come to have a friend all this way? Elise looked back at him and then moved to introduce them.

"Garrett, this is my friend Grace, I lived with her for several months in Mournstead."

Grace interrupted before she could say more. "Oh, she didn't just live with us, she rescued me! Elise came to us at a time of uncertainty in my life, I don't know how I would have gotten by without her!"

Elise glowed under her friends praise. "When you left, I had no idea where you went!"

"We weren't sure where we were going either, but when we found this village, we knew it was home! I have so much to tell you, please, can you come to my house for lunch?"

Elise looked excitedly at Garrett. "We would love to!"

The friends walked happily to Grace's home, the girls chatting the whole way, as if they had never been apart. Garrett enjoyed seeing Elise so valued and loved by her friend.

"How is Frank and little James?" She asked her friend.

A shadow came over Grace's face. "Frank passed away, shortly after we arrived here."

"Oh Grace, I am so sorry."

"Thank you, my dear. I've remarried since then, I am Grace Bancroft now. Little James is three already and," she placed a hand over her belly, "we will be adding another soon!"

Elise smiled and held her friends arm, remembering baby James and the experiences she had with her family. Grace had been the kindest and truest friend. They arrived at the door of her home and an older woman opened it. Grace introduced the woman as her housekeeper and the trio went inside.

"James? Darling, come and meet someone!"

Little footsteps were heard running into the main room, and Elise's eyes went misty when a tiny boy appeared. Grace bent down to speak to the child. "James, I want you to meet someone very special to me," his eyes looked up at the newcomers as he waited patiently for his mother's next words. "This is your Aunt Elise and her friend, Garrett."

Elise looked lovingly at her friend, feeling overjoyed ay being introduced as "Aunt." She had considered her friend a sister, and now she knew that Grace felt the same way.

James smiled sweetly and then ran from his mother's arms to Elise. "Play with me!" He cried as he tugged at her hand. She couldn't object to this request and went willingly with the boy.

Grace instructed her housekeeper to prepare a lunch for them and then turned back to Garrett. "I really don't know what I would have done without Elise."

"I believe she has mentioned you before."

Grace nodded her head. "The town we came from, it was not a pleasant place for either of us. We needed each other. I was newly married and about to have a child, no family other than my dear Frank. I was so pleased when he told me he had paid for Elise to come and stay with us. I wish more than anything I could have taken her with us when we left."

"How long was she with you?"

Grace thought back to that time in her life. "Let's see, less than a year I suppose, but it felt like she was with me for so much longer. I'm so glad to have found her again."

They had lunch together, laughing and sharing stories. The two really did seem like sisters. Garrett learned that not only was Elise present during the birth of baby James, but a vital part of it as well. Grace had become so tired after two full days of labor, she had wanted to give up. Elise helped her find the strength she needed to continue.

He was in awe of just how incredible this woman was.

After lunch, James grew tired and Grace announced that it was time for him to have a nap. This let them know it was time to go, and they parted with promises to return soon. They walked slowly back into town and went to their horses to go back to the Manor.

Chapter Eight

They spoke lightheartedly with each other until they were deep within the woods. They seemed to feel the presence of each other, and they were simply enjoying it. Something seemed to be different, something was happening. Neither of them wanted this day to end, so they rode home slowly, quietly.

Halfway home, Garrett stopped his horse and looked around. He seemed to be wrestling with an idea in his head. She waited to see what he was going to do. "May I show you something?" he asked.

"Alright." She answered.

He turned his horse and started following a new path. "It's not as smooth of a ride as this, but I'll keep you safe". He spoke so gently, he wondered if she heard.

"I know you will, Garrett."

They took a narrow path, full of flowering vines and age old greenery. Twisting and turning so many times, she wondered if this could possibly lead to anything. Still, she trusted Garrett. Probably more than she should. The horses had to step just right as to not stumble, and only someone who knew what they were doing could guide them. They finally reached a clearing in the woods. Garrett turned to see her face when she saw what only he knew about. A piece of earth virtually untouched and magnificent. Soft ground cover made up the floor, rich foliage decorated the outer edges, and a stream flowed in the most picturesque way. There were deer running freely, and the sweet smell of roses. Garrett dismounted and tied his horse to a nearby tree, then reached up to help her down. This time, she accepted the help, no longer feeling the need to prove her worth, and he lowered her into his arms and gazed into her eyes.

"I may not have much time," he thought to himself, "but perhaps I can enjoy a little of what I have left."

He looked as if he would kiss her, and she melted within his arms. She started to close her eyes to accept the kiss when he relaxed his hold on her, and then softly turned away.

"Garrett?" She asked gently. "What is this place?"

"Do you like it?" He asked wistfully.

"Oh, very much. It's beautiful." She looked over the clearing and spotted a swan making its way across the stream.

"When I was a boy, and I found out my Uncle didn't want me and I would come to live with the royal family, I was scared," he began, "the last night I was to spend in his home, I waited until my uncle was asleep, and ran away, into these woods. I must have ran for miles, I didn't stop until I ran right into this clearing. When I got here I just stopped. It was like the woods heard my cries and lead me here. I washed my face in the stream, ate the fruits from the trees, and then curled up and went to sleep right over there." He pointed to a shaded spot with thick, lush grass.

She tried to picture this tall, strong man as a small child, crying out for love and acceptance in these woods. He must have felt so unwanted. She touched his hand softly and he took it in his, grateful for the comfort she was offering. "What happened next?"

"I woke up, covered in early morning dew, surrounded by a heavy fog. I heard the sound of a woman's voice, it seemed to call out to me. I followed it for over an hour and it lead me right back to the village."

"It's a wonder you made it out safely." She observed.

"I wasn't afraid. I've always wondered if that voice was my mother's spirit, that she was keeping watch over me, guiding me to safety. I made it home before anyone noticed I was gone."

Tears came to her eyes as Elise tightened her grip on Garrett's hand. "I believe you," she whispered, "I think she still watches over you. I hope she does."

He could hear the emotion in her voice. "Do you remember your parents?" He asked.

"I never met my father." She started, "I only have faint memories of my mother. I know her hair was the same color as mine, and I remember her reading the book to me. There's not much more."

Garrett thought how much worse it must be to have nothing to remember. At least he had something of a childhood, this girl did not. How lonely they both were. She put her head down on his chest and he wrapped his arms around her. They stood in the clearing and held each other for a long time. After a while, he took her hand and led her around the forest. They stayed until they saw the evening light, and then they knew it was time to go.

As they walked back toward the horses, Garrett began to feel that his time was growing short. It was time for him to learn from her now.

"Elise," he began, slowly, timidly. "May I ask you for guidance with something?"

She was curious what possible help she could offer him, and could think of nothing. "Yes, anything."

He waited so long to begin that she wondered if he had changed his mind. "What's it like…to be alone?"

She knew now he was asking about his future. It was a future she started picturing herself in, but it was too soon to share that with him. "You and I come from a different background. No matter what happens or where you go, I don't think you will be alone for long."

Missing her passive hint, he continued. "I guess I mean, on the inside. Did you ever feel like you were alone in the world?"

This time Elise hesitated before answering. "Yes, I used to, all the time. I used to feel like if I disappeared, if I just vanished off the face of the earth, no one in the world would even notice." She looked away for a moment before turning her eyes back to him. "When I was young, I used to wonder if I was even real. I wondered why I was here, and what possible purpose I had."

Garrett nodded his head, feeling like he understood what she meant. He put her arms around her and she welcomed the embrace. Out here in these woods, he was different, freer with his emotions. "How did you get through living like that?"

She let out a long sigh. "I survived it. All I did was survive. When no one wanted me, when nothing I did was right, and when I didn't have a single person in the world to turn to, all I could do was survive." Her eyes clouded over with fear, anger; and for a brief, fleeting moment, the hopelessness that used to rule her. Then she focused her eyes on him and it all but disappeared. "But, that's not what I want for you,

Garrett. That's not what you have ahead of you. No matter what happens, I don't want you to just survive."

She paused, and Garrett lifted his eyebrows in anticipation of what she was about to say. She gently placed her hand on his face and caressed his cheek.

"I want you to live the incredible life you were meant to have."

He looked down into her eyes. She had lived with so much pain and sorrow, but all he saw in her beautiful face was acceptance, understanding, and hope. Elise saw in him what he wanted so desperately for them both; healing, safety, and confident assurance. He wished he could be the one to take all of her troubles away, even for a moment. All of the voices he had been listening to about her, everything inside of him that told him not to get too close, were suddenly very quiet.

Tightening his hold around her waist, he drew her close, and she reacted by placing her hands up and around his neck. She tipped her head back slightly, her cheeks warming and her breath heavy. He gazed from her eyes to her lips, wetting his own in anticipation. Garrett could hear a new voice in his head, a voice that came from a place in his soul that he had refused to listen to until now. He had never felt this way about anyone before. She gently lifted her lips to his and he finished closing the gap between them.

Elise melted into his kiss. For a single moment in time, they were the only two people on earth. His kiss was gentle, and she knew he was holding back. If only they could stay here, just the two of them, in this magical forest. He pulled back much too soon and Elise wished it wasn't over.

"Garrett?" She asked without knowing the question, or what his answer would be. They were both breathing heavy, their cheeks glowing with life. A million things were going through her mind. His eyes held something different now, and she held her breath, waiting for him to speak. What if he wanted to take the horses and run away with her? What if he wanted to go back to the Manor and change everything? She smiled in anticipation.

Whatever he was about to say, whatever he would ask of her, she knew what her answer would be.

He turned away, "I-I'm so sorry. Elise, I shouldn't have…."

She took a step toward him and started to place a hand on his shoulder, but he turned back towards her and spoke again before she had the chance to say anything.

"We should get back."

Elise looked at him, shocked, disappointed, and confused. Of all the things he could have said, that's not what she expected to hear.

Gathering their horses, they rode back home in silence.

Chapter Nine

"Welcome home, Stephen" Hazel met her master as his carriage stopped in front of the Manor.

"Thank you, Hazel!" He stepped out, looking worn from his journey, but content. "It's good to be back home. How is everyone?"

Hazel dismissed the coachman and followed him inside. "Well enough, Sir. Olivia has a bit of a cold, but is mending."

"Good. Tell her to take time to rest, please. I know how colds can linger." He was to his desk now and Hazel poured him a cup of tea that another servant had brought in. "What else?"

"Jones says the harvest will be near double this year."

He considered this. "Excellent. Let's arrange for the villagers to take part in the harvest, as usual. They are welcome to anything they wish." He sorted through several of the papers on his desk. "How is my guest acclimating herself?"

"Very well. Elise seems much more comfortable here now, she is learning fast. It's almost like she was born for this life." Hazel looked at Stephen with a knowing smile, he pretended not to notice. Fine. She would let him pretend for a while longer. "Of course, with Garrett at her side, they are getting along very well. Putting those two together was a wise decision." She paused for a moment until he looked up at her.

"Is there something else, Hazel?"

She smiled down at him. "There is a bit of a romance brewing between those two." She raised an eyebrow at Stephen. "But I suspect you planned that one."

Stephen paused with the news of his scheming, then smiled brightly. "I thought it was a plan, but I guess it was really just hope." He nodded his head slightly, thinking of the picture in his mind of a future he so badly wanted. "I think everything is going to be just fine."

"She's been a wonderful addition to the household. We very much enjoy her company. I think she will make him an excellent wife."

He looked up at her and chuckled. "Now Hazel, don't go giving my secrets away, you will ruin all my plans." Stephen winked at her.

"Don't you worry my dear boy, I can assure you all of your secrets are safe with me."

Hazel laughed at his scheming and excused herself for the night. Stephen sipped his tea and looked out the window, pondering the next steps toward victory. The last time he saw those two, he told Garrett to look after Elise. Tomorrow, he would ask Elise to look after Garrett.

Just then, he saw something moving outside. Within minutes he could distinguish the figures of two people on horseback, riding very close together with their hands intertwined. A huge smile spread out across the face of the prince. Everything was working according to plan. He hoped he would soon be able to tell them the truth, and acknowledge them as brother and sister. Then he would confidently take his place as the next king, with a family to help him along the way.

As the two riders reached the Manor gate, Garrett let go of Elise's hand. It was over now. It had to come to an end. He had to go back to reality. Elise would prepare to marry his friend, and he must prepare to leave. What he wouldn't give to turn back now, to ride off into the woods with Elise, and never look back. But that wasn't fair to her. Here she had the chance to be a princess, and soon, a queen. He couldn't take that away from her, she meant too much to him now. He couldn't offer her the same life that his friend could. Suddenly, the memories of the day turned into the certainty of the future, and he felt very, very tired.

"Is something wrong?" Elise noticed the change in his demeanor. Perhaps tonight was only special to her. He must have been inquiring today about a new charge. She knew he planned to leave, was he anxious? Was it that bad living at the Manor for him?

"I'm just tired, that's all" He smiled as he spoke, but it was haunted with sadness. They dropped off the horses to the groomsman and were told of the prince's homecoming. "Goodnight Elise, thank you for joining me today" he said rather dismissively. He was ready to be done with this torture, knowing what he wanted was all right here, and that it would all be taken away, was becoming too much. She barely returned his thanks when he turned and walked swiftly inside and to his room.

Elise felt a little hurt. He seemed to enjoy their time together today, but as soon as they got back to the Manor, everything changed again. So he wanted to leave, so what? He could leave. She had to start acting like a princess who would marry the prince. A prince who was now back in his home. In her home. With a sense of angry determination, Elise walked straight to Stephens's office. She might as well greet her future husband, surely he would not be so eager to dismiss her as Garrett had done.

She knocked loudly on the door of the prince's study. "Come in" was the friendly reply. She opened the door, resolved to have a nice visit with her future husband, determined to pay her attentions to someone who wanted to be with her, even if it was for the wrong reasons; but when she opened the door and tried to picture herself married to this man, a man who was still a stranger, she broke down and cried.

Stephen rushed over to her side, hardly knowing what to do for her. He led her to sit on a lounge chair and positioned himself in the one across from her. "What's the matter Elise? Has someone hurt you? Has Garrett…" his voice held a question he never thought he would have to ask.

"No, no, I'm fine, Garrett, he's…no. Please don't think that, I'm just so foolish…I'm sorry, I should go." Elise suddenly felt embarrassed to be here, crying out of frustration to the person she was really intended for.

"You will do no such thing." He spoke as though soothing a friend. "Now you sit here and let me help. He brought her a handkerchief and a hot cup of tea. He wrapped a warm shawl around her shoulders and went back to his seat. Elise wanted to laugh, in spite of her tears. How kind was he, yes, but it was not the familiar way of Garrett. Stephen was attending to her as he would a friend or family member, not a fiancé. This wasn't so bad. At least she didn't have to pretend to flirt. He retook his seat and waited patiently for her to speak.

"I'm sorry for making such a scene, it was not my intention. I was coming to see you, but not for this." Elise looked down at the floor, thoroughly spent with tears.

"I don't mind being a shoulder to cry on. I'll tell you what, next time, I'll be the one crying, and you can make me tea. Do we have a deal?" He smiled.

Elise laughed at his suggestion. It certainly was distracting. "It's a deal."

"Good. Now, would you like to tell me what's on your mind?"

She hesitated for a moment. She couldn't talk to her future husband about the intentions of his friend. She had to choose her words carefully. "It's about Garrett, he's been helping me so much, showing me around, introducing me to people, showing me how to be comfortable here…"

Stephen smiled with pride, happy his friend had taken so much initiative.

She continued. "When we are together, he makes me feel like he…enjoys my company and the time we spend together. But once we come back, a shadow comes over him, and it's as though he can't wait to get away from me."

He pondered this. "Why do you think that is?"

Elise considered the possible reasons. "Well, I imagine he is anxious to leave."

Stephens face turned white and his voice was shallow. "Leave?"

Maybe this wasn't working out according to plan after all.

Garrett flew about his room, knocking down objects that stood in his way. He tossed a pillow at the door, not seeing that it was opening, and almost hit Stephen in the face. "Watch out!" The prince shouted, catching the pillow. Garrett stood, surprised for a moment, a small amount of anger fleeing from his face just long enough for his friend to see the slight glisten of emerging tears.

"We need to talk." Said the prince to his friend. "Please?"

Out on Garrett's balcony, he stood with his arms folded, starring out into the night sky. Stephen didn't want to have this conversation. He didn't want to hear the words his friend was going to say.

"Elise tells me you are leaving?" He asked quietly.

Garrett waited a long time before answering. "I am."

Now Stephen waited to speak. "Can I ask why?"

Garrett turned around suddenly, dropping his arms to his side, and stared fiercely at the prince. His words took on a passion that Stephen had not heard before. "Are you kidding me? Are you really going to stand there and ask me why!?"

Stephen felt a lump form at his throat. This felt so foreign, and it sounded like he was to blame.

"Do you honestly think I want to be here with your new bride?" Garrett was taking a whole new liberty with his words.

Stephen was taken aback by his piercing words. How did he know? How could Garrett possibly know about Christina? She had been the one he was visiting while out of the country, but he hadn't breathed a word of it to Garrett, knowing he had enough to worry about. He had planned to confide in him once he was sure, once he knew Christina was the one, but to think he didn't want to be here once they were married confused and hurt him.

"I didn't realized you knew." He spoke tentatively.

Was this some kind of a secret? Garrett grew incredulous. Did Stephen honestly think this was a mystery? He had all but flaunted it, right in his face, taunting him that he had planned to marry Elise. "So it's really true?"

"Well, yes, sort of. I mean, I wasn't sure yet. I thought you would be pleased, I don't understand."

Garrett just stared at him. "I think it's pretty clear I'm not needed here anymore."

Stephen felt slighted. He raised his voice this time. "So that's how it is? I decide to get married, and you can't wait to run? This is just a job to you, isn't it?"

Garrett had so much he wanted to say, but he chose to stay silent, knowing that nothing either of them could say would change the situation.

"Fine. You stay just long enough for Elise to feel ready and then I want you out!"

With that, Stephen left the room, Garrett slammed the door shut, and Elise, who could hear every word from her balcony window, went to her bed to weep.

The prince stormed down to the servant's quarters and roused the housekeeper, Hazel. "What on earth is wrong, sir?"

"I'm leaving. Now, immediately."

Hazel looked at him, bewildered. "You just got back, is something wrong?"

"Just some unfinished business, it seems I have some things to do that can no longer wait. I am going back to where I came, and I won't be returning here alone. Please make the arrangements so that I can leave here as soon as possible."

Stephen went briefly to his room to pack a few things he hadn't brought with him the first time. He took out a small bag and filled it with his mother's wedding ring, his best suit, and his father's letter. He walked quickly out of his room, wanting, needing to get away. He took one final stop in his office before he left, and wrote a letter to Elise. He knew she was the only hope he had of this turning around somehow. He left the letter with Hazel, instructing her to deliver it the next day. Within the hour, without another word, he was gone.

Garrett fell in and out of sleep all throughout the long night. Tossing and turning, he was sleeping so lightly that he was awoken immediately when he heard the screams. Thinking he must have been dreaming, he tried to relax, then he heard it again and he knew.

It was Elise.

He could hear her screaming from the wall that was between their rooms. His heart raced with fear and he quickly got up and ran to her door. The screaming grew louder as he fumbled with the handle, his eyes still foggy from sleep and his mind racing with uncertainty. He finally managed to open the door, picturing the worst.

What he saw was something that turned his fears into confusion and sadness.

Elise was alone, screaming in her sleep. He went to her side and tried to calmly wake her from what must have been a terrible dream. He shook her very gently and quietly called for her to wake up. She continued to thrash about and scream, and it sounded like pure agony to Garrett. He leaned over her, put his hands on both of her shoulders, shook hard, and yelled; pleading, for her to wake up.

"Wake up, please, wake up! Elise!" He shouted.

Suddenly, the screaming stopped. The sounds of distress turned into open sobs of terror and relief. She sat up and put her arms around Garrett's chest, holding on to him as if he would disappear if she let go. She shook and sobbed in his arms as he rocked her gently, soothing her with calm words of assurance and safety.

"It's alright, it's over now. I'm here, you're safe here with me." He repeated this over and over until she stopped shaking, her arms loosened and her sobs quieted. Tenderly he caressed her hair and kissed her forehead. It felt so natural to hold her, he never wanted to let go.

She could hear his heart beating in his chest. It sounded as fast as her own. She felt protected like this, wrapped in his arms. "Will you stay with me? Please, Garrett?" Realizing that might be too much to ask, she quickly added, "Just until I fall asleep?" She was scared. Scared and alone and she needed him. Of course he would stay. He would do just about anything she asked of him tonight.

He laid down next to her in the bed and held her close, letting his former anger and frustration disappear, just for tonight. Tomorrow, he would go back to hopelessness and despair; but tonight, he would just hold on to the woman he was falling in love with.

Chapter Ten

The next morning, beautiful sunlight shone through the balcony window and found Elise's sweet face. It beckoned her to wake, and she turned to find the figure of someone sleeping next to her. Surprise turned to gratefulness when she remembered the previous night. Maybe it was childish to ask him to stay. She thought surely he would leave the moment she was back to sleep, but here he was. He stayed all night to watch over her, to keep her demons from harming her. She felt so safe like this, nestled in his warm embrace. He told her yesterday in the woods that he would keep her safe, if only she could keep him near her. She remembered his words on the balcony last night. Then, ridding them from her mind, she decided that she would consider his words another time. This morning, they were the only two people that mattered.

She felt him stir and she softly brushed the hair from his forehead. He slowly opened his eyes and found her gentle, soothing face. He wished he could stay here, close to her, forever. "Good morning" he said, his voice heavy with sleep. He smiled and pulled her closer to him. She welcomed the embrace. "Good morning," she echoed, almost a whisper, afraid to break this magical spell.

The events that brought him here last night came back to him, and he needed to know. "Elise, what were you dreaming about last night?"

She didn't want to think about that. She just wanted to stay here, where she was safe and happy, where she felt alive and free. "Several things." She stated, almost blank, afraid to say the words.

"Please tell me." He urged. She looked into his eyes and saw the worry he held for her. No matter what was going on, she really did feel safe with him.

"What do you know about my life before I came here?" She asked.

Garrett gathered his thoughts. "I know you were in service, you went from house to house, and the people you worked for were not very kind to you." He brushed his fingers against her shoulder as he spoke, as if his touch could heal her wounds.

She cleared her throat before speaking. "The people who usually wanted me were families, people with young children to care for, or elderly people who needed help caring for themselves. But the last home I worked in, it was different." She paused and looked at him, wondering if she could really let him in like this, sharing the deepest darkest parts of herself. "It was just one man, Mr. Devlin. I knew of him before I went to live in his house, he had a reputation for being coarse, and violent. I thought that if I just stayed quiet, did my job, I would be ok. But that wasn't the case. "

"Every day and every night, he drank. And with each day his attentions to me grew worse. It started with little things. He would throw a teacup at me if the tea I made him was too hot or too cold. Then he started throwing books if he couldn't find the one he was looking for. Sometimes he would grab me or push me. On better days he tried to convince me to go to bed with him. He said he would make my life better if I did. I refused him each time, and then the violence would get worse."

Elise wiped a single tear from her eyes before continuing. "The last day I was there, he was so angry that he went to the kitchen and got a knife. He told me that I had one last chance. I could be his mistress, or he would end my life, right there. That's when the guards found me and demanded my release. If they hadn't shown up when they did, it would have all been over."

Garrett was horrified. This sweet, angelic woman that he held now in his arms, was tortured, manipulated, and harmed, in the name of service. He felt a fire in his soul and vowed to find a way to put a stop to this mistreatment of servants somehow. He wished he could go and find that man, and stop him from harming anyone, ever again. "I'm so sorry Elise, I had no idea it was so bad. You must have nightmares every night."

"Yes, I do have them each night, but last night, it was worse." Elise whispered, for now she was pulled so close to him that she could barely breathe.

Garrett couldn't imagine something worse. He braced himself to hear what she would say next.

"Last night I dreamt that you were leaving, and I tried to make you stay, but nothing I said mattered to you. You were leaving, and Stephen said it was my fault, and that I should go back to where I came from. He made me leave, and gave me back to that horrible, evil man. You were there, and I was holding on to you, begging you to keep me safe from him, and you pushed me away. All I could see was a knife raised above my head and I just screamed and screamed, and then I woke up."

At this point, they were both crying. Holding each other, and crying. Her words pierced his soul. "Elise, I promise you, no matter what happens, I will always protect you."

She looked up at him, her eyes, pleading. "But you won't be here! You're going to leave!"

He hugged her tighter, his tears turning to desire, "Somehow, I promise, I'll never let anything happen to you, never!"

His words overtook her and they kissed each other. Instead of the soft, stolen kiss from the forest yesterday, it was a fervent, all-consuming embrace. There was a hunger in each of them that could not be satisfied. Time stood still, and in this moment, there was just the two of them, intertwined in each other's arms. The love and desire they felt for each other was quickly coming to the surface. He held her and kissed her so ardently that they didn't hear the knock at her bedroom door.

Elise broke free from his grasp when she heard the second knock. "Someone's at the door" she whispered. Suddenly they became aware of how wildly inappropriate it would be if someone found them like this. He held a finger over his lips and then let go of her. She quickly moved across her room to the door. Without opening in, she asked, "Who is it?"

"Elise? It's Hazel, dear. Are you alright?"

"I'm not feeling well this morning Hazel, just didn't sleep well last night."

"I understand, dear. I've brought you a tray. I'll just leave it here at the door and you can get it in a bit."

"Thank you, Hazel." She said quietly.

Garrett watched her. As Elise stood at the door, he felt a longing that he didn't allow himself to acknowledge before today. He wanted her. Body, mind, and soul, he wanted this woman. He rose from the bed and walked over to her from behind. By the time the maid was gone, his arms were wrapped around her waist, pulling her close and kissing her neck. She turned around and let him kiss her for what seemed like forever, not wanting it to end. This time, her hands went around his waist and his hands explored her hair. She felt a need within her to continue, but she also knew they had to stop, before anything more happened.

She started to pull away and he only drew her closer. Elise broke the trance they were in by pushing slightly on his arms.

He immediately halted his advances and looked down at her face, searching for an explanation. She looked into his eyes, and knew how easily she could get lost there. "We have to stop. You know we do." She smiled. "At least let's see if there's any tea on that tray."

Garrett breathed her in deeply, and then let her go. She opened the door and he grabbed the tray. Setting it on the table, he had to laugh. "I think we've been found out" he said to her. There were two cups, and two breakfast plates on the tray. He winked at her and she blushed, softly. "Well as long as you are here, and so is your breakfast, you might as well stay for a while."

Garrett brought the tray to a table on her balcony. They each took a blanket to wrap around their shoulders, and went outside to eat. They sat across from each other, enjoying the warm breeze, each other's company, and the thrill of this stolen moment of bliss.

"Elise," he said, "There's a letter here." He picked it up from the tray and handed it to her. He admired her while she sipped her tea with one hand and read her letter with the other.

"Dear Elise,

I'm sorry to run off so soon, but there is an urgent matter I must attend to. I don't know how long I will be gone, but when I get back, I hope to begin preparations for a wedding. I'd like to be married before the winter, and I know that these things take time, so I hope to arrive home soon. Please take care of Garrett for me while I am gone, I fear he will be leaving us soon, and you are the only one who can talk him into staying. I have so much to tell you both when I get back, I hope to see you soon, and to be united once and for all as family, as we should be.

Stephen."

Elise dropped her teacup and it shattered against the balcony floor. The color in her face drained and she thought she would be sick. Garrett rushed to her side. "What is it? What's wrong?" She could only hand him the letter so he could read it himself.

He read it quickly, then crumpled it in his hands. "What are we going to do?" she asked him.

He stood silent for the longest time, and when he spoke, his words were cold, his expression, numb. "The only thing we can do," he said softly, "prepare."

"Prepare? For what?"

"You and I both know what." He said sadly. "Stephen was clear on what he expects from us."

"You want me to go through with it, then?" There was shock in her voice. "But you said, this morning, you said you would protect me."

He held her in his arms again, and they both knew it would be the last time. "I said I would protect you, and I will. From a lifetime of regret." He kissed her forehead, gave her a sad smile, and then left the room. Elise just sat there frozen on the balcony, wondering if she could face the prince again, knowing that she was in love with his best friend.

Chapter Eleven

"Stephen, do you have any idea what you've done?!" Christina sat with him in her family's courtyard, enjoying a picnic lunch, his mother's ring glistening on her finger. He had been courting her for months now, and although she was a little surprised to see him so soon after he left, she welcomed him with joy. She said "Yes" before he had a chance to even open the ring box, and he forgot about the hurtful words of his friend in the loving arms of his new fiancé.

"What? What have I done?" Stephen reached into the picnic basket, looking for an apple. They had spent the day reading his father's letter and talking about everything that was happening when Christina stopped him, mid-sentence.

"My dear, you've made them think Elise is your intended bride! Don't you see? Garrett must think he is training her to be his permanent replacement, and that you don't want him as a companion anymore." Christina seemed to understand all of this confusion.

Stephen found the apple he had been searching for, then turned his attention back to her. "Well he's not my companion anymore, he hasn't been for a very long time. Garrett is my friend, for a long time he was my best friend. So he's right, I don't want him as a companion and I am taking a wife." He kissed her cheek, but she continued to try and make him see what was happening, and why his world was out of sorts.

"But, he doesn't see it that way. You told him Elise was your cousin."

He leaned back onto his elbow and took a bite. He thought about what she was saying and tried to think back on the last couple of months. "But I only said that so she wouldn't feel like she had to stay. I wanted her to stay because she wanted to, not because she thought it was her duty."

Christina shook her head at him, her golden curls bouncing softly under her hat. "You just don't understand the mess you have made. Garrett thinks Elise is intended for you. No wonder he's been so sad since she arrived. How would you feel if he told you he didn't want to be your friend anymore, and that he wanted you to teach someone else how to take your place?"

"I just thought, if I got them to spend some time together, they would at least be friends." Stephen began solemnly, "When my Father died, I felt like Garrett was the only true friend I had left. I would have been all alone if it wasn't for him, and I knew what would happen if I didn't find a way for him to stay. He should have left years ago, made his own life. Once I turned 18, I knew eventually he would leave. But by then, he was more than my companion, he was a brother."

"Why didn't you tell him about your sister?" Christina chided.

"Because…because I didn't want him to build a wall between himself and Elise. At first I kept it a secret to give her time, but the first day she was with us, I saw a spark. It was like they were meant for each other. So, I made a plan, to elevate Elise to her birthright and keep my friend from leaving."

Christina looked lovingly at her fiancé. "But your plans didn't work out the way you'd hoped."

Stephen smiled at her words. "Yes, I suppose I did make a mess of things. I don't know if I can fix it. Garrett seems to hate me now, I'm not completely sure why."

"I think," she said to him, "he is in love with Elise."

Suddenly, the last few months became clear. The anger and passion from Garrett, the tears from Elise, and the last words they said to each other. He was so ashamed of the way he had handled things. If only he hadn't of kept her true identity a secret. If only he had been truthful with them from the start.

Then, he had an idea. "Christina, my love, how would you like to help me make things right for our future family members?"

She smiled at him, ready for an adventure. "With pleasure."

Garrett and Elise spent their remaining time in the company of others. He said it was to get her used to talking to people, but she knew it was to keep them distanced from each other. She did the things he asked of her willingly, but there was always pain behind every completed task. She felt truly lifeless now. Each day she wanted to be with Garrett more and more, and each day he dutifully stepped farther away from her. She had to find a way to let him go, after all, he had chosen loyalty to his friend over the love he felt for her.

So the final days passed with bitterness and desire, longing for forbidden love, until one day she was so sick of everything that was going on, thinking of the prospects of her future and knowing it would be a future without Garrett. Elise ran out of the Manor in a fury of tears, determined to get away. She ran until she got to the stables, found a horse, and rode out to the woods; knowing she needed some time to think. She went so fast, that she didn't see Garrett, sitting low in an empty stall.

He heard her come in, knew where she was going, and why, and if her head was spinning with grief and anger like his was, he knew what he had to do. He would follow her, into the clearing he showed her that day, into the place where there was still a little bit of magic in their sad, lonely world, and he would try to comfort her for what they both felt would happen very soon.

Elise remembered the path she had taken with Garrett. She led her horse swiftly across the narrow way until she reached the most beautiful part of the forest. Once she reached it, the tears began to flow, angry and hopeless. She fell down on her knees and wept so violently that she didn't hear Garrett approach. He knelt down beside her and put his arms around her, and the two of them held each other through their sobs.

After their tears had been spent, she looked up at him, softly wiping her red hot cheeks. "What happens now?"

Garrett was tired. So very tired. He looked down at the woman he loved, but couldn't have. "I've been thinking about that for a long time. I know I have to leave, and I'm not sure if I will be able to come back."

Elise sat back, wishing he hadn't said the words. "When?" She had so much she wanted to say, if only they had more time, if only they were free.

Garrett braced himself for her reaction. "Tomorrow, at first light. Everything is ready."

She didn't want to hear this, didn't want him to say these terrible words. "But you can't leave, I'm not ready to do this alone."

He smiled sadly at her. In the months they had known each other, she went from being little more than a frightful child to a woman of strength and ability. "Elise, you are ready. You will lead your people with grace, kindness, and wisdom, I have no doubt. And you won't be alone."

He took a letter from his pocket and showed it to her. "Stephen sent me this. He will be here tomorrow morning. Elise, I can't be here when he comes back, I can't sit back and watch him be with you. Do you trust me?"

"Of course I trust you," she said truthfully, "I love you."

Garrett took in the sweet words she spoke. He looked into her eyes, so full of love, but mixed with sadness and heartbreak. "I love you too."

Suddenly, she was on her feet, "Then stay with me! Fight for me! I don't want a life with him, a hollow, fake marriage! I want you!"

He rose to stand next to her, taking both of her hands in his. "I want you too, Elise, but don't you understand? Don't you see, this is the best that I can give you? I'm leaving you here with him because I love you. You'll be a queen. I couldn't live with myself if I took that away from you. This is the way it has to be."

Elise stared at him for a long time, then turned and walked back to the horses.

They rode back to Highfield together. The sun was setting and it gave everything a dreamy, rose-like appearance. They both had so much they wanted to say, but at this point, they knew it would only bring each other pain. When they got the Manor gate, he once again helped her down from her horse, and held her for just a slight moment. But it was enough to convey his feelings for her, and the sorrow in his heart.

She took his hand and led him wordlessly to her bedroom door. "Elise," he began, "I must go."

Looking up into his eyes, she gently pulled him closer. "Stay with me, just until I fall asleep, so I don't have any bad dreams. Please, Garrett?"

It wasn't a question, it was a command. She needed to spend these last few moments beside him. She needed to feel close to him, before he was taken out of her life. He nodded and they went inside.

The next morning, when Elise woke up to the feeling of warm sunshine, she turned to find her love, but he was gone. She gently placed her hand over his pillow, and knew nothing would ever be the same.

Chapter Twelve

Elise tried her best to stop crying long enough to great her future husband. His carriage had been spotted and her presence had been requested. She knew what he expected of her, and she must try to be a dutiful wife and queen, to honor the wishes of the man she loved.

The carriage stopped and Stephen stepped out. He smiled at her with genuine regard, and she braced herself to accept his greeting. But instead of going to her, he turned back to the carriage and helped a woman to step out. She was beautiful. Blonde curls, a polished appearance, and a cheerful smile. He offered her his arm and she took it without question. Elise didn't know what to think as they approached her.

"Elise, my dear, allow me to introduce Christina," the woman he referred to smiled kindly at her, eyes shining, "My wife."

Garrett had kept his word and left at the first sign of daylight, before Stephen would arrive at the Manor.

He took almost nothing with him, a few changes of clothes, the money he had earned in his time with the family, and a riding coat. Looking around his room at the trove of mementos he had treasured from the last 13 years, he let out a heavy sigh, and shook his head in defeat. Taking anything more would just serve as a daily reminder of what he had left behind.

Going out to the stables to get Raven, he gave a final look to the balcony window where he knew his love slept, then turned and left as swiftly as he could, eager to start his mission. If he couldn't be part of her future, he could at least help heal her past.

Stopping in town at the messenger's home, he went inside and stood expectantly. Tom was ready with the papers he had requested. His earlier visit with Elise had brought him there to look for housing in nearby villages, but he had changed his request weeks later. He needed to know all the information he could about Mournstead, the village where Elise had lived. He had sent money ahead to purchase a house and furnishings, just enough for a few weeks. There was business he must attend to there, before he decided where he would start a new life. Maybe by then he could forget her, let her go and try to find some sort of purpose in the sad and lonely life that await.

As he took a last look at Westmore, the village he was born in, he mentally said his goodbyes. He wasn't just leaving the woman he loved, he was leaving his home, his memories, his past, and any prospects of a happy future. He was leaving everything he had ever known, with no chance of finding happiness ever again.

"Gone? What do you mean?" Stephen's marital bliss turned to shock at hearing the news.

Hazel held on to Elise as she sobbed. "It's true sir, very early this morning. I asked him to wait for you, but he wanted to be gone before you got back."

"It's too late," Stephen thought to himself, "it's already too late." He looked back at his new wife, her sorrowful expression made it even worse. He came home expecting to tell everyone good news, to right the wrongs that he didn't fully know he was making. Now, he saw the things he worked so hard for slip away from his grasp. He turned to Elise and took her hands in his, tears forming in his eyes.

"Elise, forgive me, this is all my fault."

She left the motherly embrace of Hazel to face him. "I don't understand, Garrett thought all this time that I was the one you had planned to marry. Wasn't that the reason you brought me here?"

Stephen shook his head. "You have it all wrong, please, Elise, please forgive me!"

Christina stepped in to try to explain. "He did want you to be part of the family, dear, but not as his wife. Stephen's father left him a letter to read after he died, telling him all about you."

Stephen reached into his pocket and retrieved a handkerchief, handing it to Elise.

Elise accepted it, dried her eyes and looked at them with confusion. "Stephen's fa- the king? How did the king know anything about me?" She looked at Stephen, then looked down at the handkerchief she was using. Something about it looked so familiar to her, the fabric, the stitching, even the letters. If she hadn't known better, she would have thought it was the one she had now in her room, left behind from a father she never knew. "Where did you get this?" She handed it back to him, a chill suddenly going over her spine.

Stephen took back the precious fabric and looked down at it, running his thumb over the letters embroidered on the corner. "It's one of the king's old handkerchiefs, I keep one with me when I travel, right next to mine."

Elise felt like everything was going in slow motion. She tried to wrap her head around how that was possible. "It can't be, I have the same one, and it looks just like that. My mother said that it was my father's….."

Christina gave her husband a gentle look, pressing him to continue, and he nodded in agreement. He took Elise's hands in his own once again. She searched his eyes for an explanation and waited for what seemed like ages before he finally spoke.

"My father met your mother sometime after the queen passed away. They……spent some time together. She didn't know who he was, and when she found out, she told him to go back to his family. He didn't know she was pregnant at the time, with you."

Her eyes grew wide and she stepped back in disbelief. "I don't…..but that's impossible! That would mean I'm…."

"You're my half-sister, Elise." Stephen felt a weight lifting off of his shoulders as he finally spoke the words he had so longed to say. It felt amazing to say it, even in his grief over Garrett leaving.

Elise looked at him, her face full of confusion. What was he saying to her? She tried desperately to replay the words he had spoken in her mind, willing them to make sense. Could it be true? Suddenly, everything became clear. This is why she was brought here. This is why she looked so much like Stephen. "I have a brother?" Her tears turned to joyous laughter as she threw her arms around him. "I have a brother! I have a family!"

He hugged her tight, relieved with her acceptance of him. He couldn't possibly realize the depth of her relief at hearing this news. Not only was she not losing her freedom, but she had gained a family.

"I've wanted to tell you so many times!" He held on to her, afraid to let go. "I was so scared you wouldn't want me as a brother. My parents left, Garrett left, and I thought if you knew, you would leave too."

She held him even tighter after hearing this, then pushed him back enough to look in his eyes. "I'm not going anywhere, I'm not going to leave you, and if Garrett only knew the truth, I know he would want to stay. We'll find him, bring him back to us….."

Brother and sister began to form a plan to find Garrett and bring him back to his home and his family. They walked toward Stephen's office to try and figure out what to do next. Christina began to follow them, eager to help in any way she could, when Hazel beckoned her over. She invited her to sit at a bench a few feet away, and waited until Elise and Stephen were out of earshot before she spoke. Christina seemed to understand the need and waited patiently to see what the housekeeper had to say.

"There's something you should know, Mistress. How much do you know about the time Stephen's father was away?"

Christina thought back to what he had told her, and tried to recall every detail. From what she heard, the king must have been gone for several months.

"I'm afraid it was much longer and more tragic than that. You see, the queen died just hours after Stephen's birth, from an infection. She never even got to hold him. As soon as the king found out, he was so distraught that he left, but it wasn't for a few months, it was for over two years."

Christina couldn't believe this. "Years?!" How could that be? How could he have left his son alone for such a long time?

"Stephen feels a deep sense of abandonment, but he hasn't put the pieces together enough to fully understand why. He didn't have either of his parents, for the first two years of his life. The king was so ashamed of himself, he spent the rest of his life trying to make up for things with his son, but he never told him the truth."

Now she understood why he thought everyone was leaving him, and why he was trying so hard to rebuild a family. Having only servants to care for you for that long, not knowing his mother or father, it left a mark on him.

"Thank you for telling me this, Hazel. All of this makes much more sense now."

Several days ride gave Garrett time to think about what he was going to do. A new direction for his spiteful anger, everything he was thinking and feeling now directed to a man he had the right to hate. The farther he rode away from Elise, the harder his heart was becoming. The man who had wanted to defile and destroy such an innocent creature would finally be made accountable for the things he had done. Garrett's blood boiled as he recounted what Elise had told him. He pictured storming into that evil man's house, pulling him out into the open streets, and publicly shaming him for his sins. Or, perhaps he would arrive with a fleet of lawmakers to demand a harsh sentence.

Garrett heard a tiny voice inside of him and paused to listen. "Or, I will just find a way to stop him…permanently."

He traveled each day, stopping at night to eat and sleep at many of the various inns, purposely taking a different way than Elise and the guards had previously traveled, not wanting to be found. He soon arrived at the village of Mournstead, where Elise was from. There was a small main stretch of town with a few basic shops, nothing like Westmore village. It was dismal, just enough to make due, and nothing more. He rode about the town, picturing that worn and battered girl that first came to them living in this tiny, joyless village. He made his way to the center, asking a few people now and then some simple questions. It was easy to find where he wanted to go in a village so small.

Soon enough, he arrived at the doorstep of Mr. Devlin, the man that wanted to steal the life and soul of the woman who held his heart. He took a slow, deep breath, willing himself to go through with his devastating plan. Garrett could hear his own heart pounding deeply in his chest, his stomach in knots thinking about the things this man had done to her, the things he would have done. He didn't fully know what was about to happen, what he was truly willing to do, but he knew he had to face him, for Elise. With a fire in his soul to do the one thing left he could for her, he shook the doubt from his mind and knocked.

A servant girl opened the door, she looked no more than fifteen. She had bruises on her arms, a sullen, hollow look to her pale face. She looked as if she held a secret and he wondered if she had been treated in the same way as Elise. He burned with the very idea, and his hatred for this man grew with even more passion. Garrett asked to see her master, and she cautiously let him in.

The girl looked nervous, uneasy, as she led him inside. Garrett thought about what might have happened to Elise if she had stayed here with this man, and his former doubt about what he had to do vanished. He knew now that he had to stop him. Stop him from hurting anyone ever again. Stop him from haunting the dreams of his beloved.

The servant girl stepped slowly, quietly. She stopped at one of the doors and pointed to the room her master was in. Garrett could feel his anger rising, so close now. He opened the door with rage, but what he saw made him instantly sick. In a chair by the window, covered in flies, sat a dead man.

The smell of old liquor and decay turned his stomach and he ran out of the house. His head was spinning as he emptied his stomach onto the grass. Mr. Devlin had died at some point in the last several days, and no one had cared enough to find him. He had died in a cloud of his own evilness, without a single soul to miss him. All the things he had done to others over the years had finally caught up to him, and the price he paid for it was dear.

Clearing his head and recovering from the sickness, he went back inside and asked the girl what happened. He told her he was coming to stop him, so she needn't be afraid of telling him the truth. She told him her name was Clara, and that she had only been in this home a short time. She recalled how her master had drank himself to death, and that she was scared to tell anyone in fear that she would be blamed. Garrett told her that she didn't need to be afraid anymore. Someday, he hoped to tell the same to Elise.

"You say you've only been here a short time?"

Clara nodded her head. "Yes, my parents died several months ago, and I was living with our neighbor, but she couldn't afford to keep me anymore. She told me that Mr. Devlin had lost his servant, and agreed to take me in. I've been here several months now."

Garrett felt so sad for her, she just wanted a home. She must have come here a few months after Elise left. He pointed to the bruises on her arms. "Did he do that to you?"

She nodded her head, "Yes, the beatings got worse when I told him about the baby."

Baby? Garrett was confused. What baby? It was then than he noticed how her hands were placed protectively over her belly. He remembered the ultimatum that Mr. Devlin had given Elise, and he knew Clara had done what she had to do in order to stay alive.

He thought for several minutes about what needed to be done now. He gave her enough money to get to Glendale, the neighboring town, and asked if she would stay at the inn and wait for him for a few days. She agreed and quickly left. Garrett arranged to have Mr. Devlin removed and buried.

Feeling the weight of everything that had happened was overwhelming. He went to his newly purchased house and sat down in an unfamiliar chair, seeking comfort and time to process. He came into Mournstead to possibly do something terrible, but ended up freeing someone who had gone through the same treatment as Elise. It was quite the change in direction and Garrett was thankful for what he was able to do, as well as what he was spared from doing.

Once he had recovered, he went to the town leaders and offered to pay for everything. He wanted the house emptied and burned to the ground. The leaders were happy to oblige, knowing the terror that had gone on in that house. They told him that more than one servant girl had been found dead in the man's home, but that Mr. Devlin had always found a way out of the blame. They knew he was an evil man, but could do little to prove it.

"What would you like done with the land once it's cleared, Sir?" One of the men asked him.

Thinking of what could possibly go in its place baffled him for a moment. It wasn't enough to remove the evil, it needed to be replaced with something good. Something that changed things, something that brought hope instead of despair. "I have an idea" he told them.

Several days later, he rode his horse up to the inn Clara had settled in. She was happy to see him, and looked much improved over the short period of time. With proper care, she was beginning to regain her health. Garrett wanted to help and protect her the way he wished he could have protected Elise. He arranged for Clara to come and stay with him, so she would have a safe place to live while she waited for the baby to be born, and she was relieved to hear it, not knowing where she would go now that Mr. Devlin was gone.

He told her to take a carriage the next day to that address and he would have a room ready for her. He wished someone had taken Elise in like this when she needed help, and was happy to try and do something for this poor girl.

He rode back into the village and found the small ranch and few horses Elise must have learned to ride on. The man who owned the ranch remembered the girl, no more than 13 when she started riding. She was gentle but confident with the horses and learned to ride quickly. Picturing her here, in one of the few places she was ever happy, made him ache for her.

"First she would just come to watch, but eventually she started volunteering to care for the horses in exchange for riding lessons." He explained.

Garrett smiled as he heard the word "lessons", remembering the lesson she didn't need from him, the one she let him teach out of the merriment in her heart. If only he could go back to that day.

"Which one was her favorite?" He asked the man.

"She learned to ride all of them eventually, but once she was confident enough to go out on her own, she would usually choose this one." He led him to a stall that held a beautiful brown mare. It was such a contrast to his Raven.

"What's her name?" He asked as he greeted the horse.

The man smiled and tilted his head towards her. "This is 'Autumn', named after the season we found her in. She was a wild horse with a broken leg, close to death when we came upon her. My team brought her here and helped her heal before winter set in. She fit so well here that we knew it was her home."

Garrett could see how Elise would be drawn to her. He paid the man to board his horse, knowing he would be staying longer than he originally planned, and requested the stall next to Autumn. It seemed only natural to put them together.

The next afternoon, Clara arrived to the house Garrett had purchased. He greeted her kindly and showed her around the home and the room he had prepared for her. He told her he had also hired a housekeeper from the inn, Florence, to come and stay with them, and also to help take care of her.

"I thought…..I assumed I would be the one working here for you." Clara said to him, surprised.

Garrett tried to explain that he wanted to provide her with a safe home for her and her child, and that he wanted her to rest, heal, and build up her strength before the baby came, and that as long as he could help it, she would never be a servant again.

Tears began to well up in her eyes as she took in the words he said to her. "I don't understand, why are you being so kind to me?"

He hesitated before answering. "Because I once loved someone who went through a similar experience as you, and I wish someone would have been there, to save her from it."

Over the next few weeks, Garrett, Clara, and Florence got to know each other better. Garrett treated them both like family, and did his best to make the ladies feel comfortable. Clara seldom left the house, and allowed herself very few visitors.

This was understood by Garrett, as she both wanted and needed time to heal from the indescribable trauma she had endured. He arranged for a midwife from Glendale to come and check on her weekly, who assured them all that mother and child were both doing better.

Florence had proved to be a wise and faithful housekeeper. A woman in her fifties, she had lived in Glendale all of her life, working as an assistant in several respectable shops before working at the inn. She was a widow, and had been unable to have children, naturally making her a motherly figure for young Clara. Florence was kind and caring to her, and was delighted when Clara became her shadow, learning household duties and becoming as dear to her as she imagined her own daughter would have been.

Garrett spent most of his time out of the house. He left before sunrise and didn't get back home until after sunset. He focused on his mission every day, trying to make this village better, safer for those that lived here. Never tiring, and doing a great deal of work himself, they had built a school, several shops, a community area, and had repaired and rejuvenated many of the houses. There was very little he did for himself, he barely slept or ate. All he thought about was making things right for Elise, so that one day the hauntings of her past would heal. He wanted her to be at peace, he wanted her to be happy. Isn't that why he left? To heal her troubled past since he could not be part of her future?

No, he admitted, that wasn't why he really left. He left because he knew he couldn't offer her the same life that Stephen would. The life of a queen was so much better in his mind than what he could give her. How could she be happy with him, living a simple, everyday life, knowing what she could have had? How could he live with himself, taking away the intended bride of his best friend?

He thought about Stephen, and he missed him. Not just his presence, but his company, his friendship. Everything that had happened over the last year; the death of the king, falling in love, feeling the end of the life he knew, and leaving everyone and everything behind, tore the two friends apart. It wore on him, each day he was in this village, each day he spent away.

It was late fall when Garrett came here, and now, winter was nearing its end. He had been residing in this house for many months now, feeling a strange sense of comfort within his walls. Garrett counted back the time and was shocked to realize four months had passed. In that time, he helped build this village up to a more respectable standard. Because of its growth, Garrett convinced the village of Mournstead to merge into the larger town of Glendale, assuring that the town he had worked so hard for would continue to flourish. So much had changed and a new precedent had been set on how orphans and servants were treated. If Elise was living here now, she would not have faced the hardships that she had before. The only thing that allowed him any sleep at all was the fact that no child would ever again go through what she did.

Chapter Thirteen

Garrett came home one night to some fantastic news. Florence had grown so attached to Clara, that she asked Garrett what he thought about her adopting the sweet girl.

"You know I never had children of my own, and Clara has been such a gift to me. I don't know what I would do without her now, and I have just enough saved to buy a small house for us."

He took her hand and squeezed it gently. "I can think of no better mother for her, Florence. You have cared for both of us as if we were already family, and I know you will love Clara, and her baby, with all of your heart."

She glowed with his praise. "Thank you, dear."

They both went to Clara to ask what she thought about it, and were pleased with her gleeful response. She told Florence that she already saw her as her mother, and would be overjoyed at giving her baby such an amazing grandmother. They went to sign the papers the very next day, with Garrett's help and blessing, and received the very best gift once everything was final.

"What you went through was terrible. No one should ever have to go through the pain you have endured, but now that we have come together, and allowed ourselves time to heal, we can make something beautiful from the pain." Garrett presented Florence with a deed to a house in Glendale, big enough for both ladies and the baby, and the rest of his earnings into an account for Clara.

"This is too much!" Florence shouted, tears of joy flowing from her eyes.

Clara reached her arms out to Garrett and hugged him tight. "How can I ever thank you for everything you have done for us?"

He was reminded of a time, months ago, in a forbidden forest. Elise spoke words of encouragement to him, and he knew exactly what to say now. "I want you to live. Not just survive, but to live the incredible life you were meant to have."

Garrett hired a crew to come and gather their things for the move. He wanted to make sure Clara was settled into her permanent home before her baby was born. Once everything was ready, they took a carriage to their new residence. It was a lovely yellow house, with many windows to allow lots of sunshine. They knew this house would soon be filled with the life both Florence and Clara had previously been denied, and they were thankful for their new beginning.

Clara walked cautiously through each room, and tried to imagine her baby here. She knew the time was coming very soon, and she was glad that she would no longer need to move. Walking into one of the bedrooms, she found all of her things from Garrett's house had been carefully placed inside, and at the other side of the room was a beautiful, handmade, wooden cradle.

"Garrett!" She cried. "Did you do this?!"

He came running at the sound of his name and went quickly into her room, fearing something was wrong. Seeing Clara standing before the cradle, he smiled. "Do you like it?"

She hugged him tight. "I love it, thank you!"

Florence came in behind them. "Look inside, dear."

Clara let go of Garrett and turned her attention back to the cradle. Inside she found a delicately crocheted baby blanket, hat, and tiny socks. "When did you make these, Mother?"

She relished the sound of Clara calling her that. She spent her whole life wishing to hear it, fearing her time was gone forever. Clara asked to give her that name the night she asked to adopt her, and it became sweeter each time she heard it.

"A little each night, after you went to sleep. We wanted them to be a surprise."

She gently touched the lovely things her baby would soon use. "Thank you both, for everything."

Garrett stayed at the new house long enough to make sure everything had been taken care of. Both the midwife and the doctor would be ready at a moment's notice to come to the house, and special instructions were given to the city to make sure they were well cared for. He knew it would soon be time for him to move on and find his permanent home, somewhere far away from anything that reminded him of Elise.

Upon reaching his house that night, he found a letter that came for him from his Uncle's lawyer. It said he had died at sea many months ago. Garrett didn't know how to feel about this. Perhaps he should feel an overwhelming sadness that yet another person connected to him was lost. Why he would have even been contacted was a mystery, as his Uncle had never once wrote to him. As he read on, the reason for the letter suddenly became clear. He had left Garrett everything he owned. Several large ships and trading companies, an estate in Westmore village, and enough money to live at leisure for the rest of his life. He had to read the letter three times in disbelief, and then sat back in his chair and laughed.

He, who had spent every penny he had ever earned rebuilding this village, to give what little he had of himself in some small way to the love of his life, was now a very wealthy man.

"Why Garrett," Florence said as she opened her front door, "You know you needn't knock." She led him into the front room where Clara was lounging, and offered him tea as he sat down.

"Yes, thank you, but first, I must tell you both something very important." He was wringing his hands in anticipation, looking at them with a mixture of nervousness and excitement.

Clara sat up straighter and Florence sat next to her, they instinctively took each other's hands, wondering what news had him so flustered. He told them about his uncle's letter. They listened with shock, delighted to hear of his good fortune.

"No one deserves this more than you, my dear." Florence said with a smile.

Clara clapped her hands in joy. "Certainly not, you are a hero, and a saint."

He shook his head and leaned forward, hanging his head down. "No, I don't deserve this. Far from it I'm afraid." Now he told them both about his past, never having shared it with them before now. He told them about Stephen and his time at Highfield, and about Elise. "I behaved wrongly toward her, and then I came here to possibly do something unforgivable."

"But you didn't, don't you see?" Clara gently tucked her hand into his. "You did something wonderful. And I don't believe you were wrong in your feelings for her."

Garrett let out a heavy sigh at her redeeming words.

"Do you still love her?" Florence asked softly.

He looked across the room at a small painting of a single, blooming rose. "Yes."

Clara smiled at him and Florence nodded her head. "Then don't you know what it is you have to do?"

A few days later, he checked Raven out of the stable with a plan. He would go back to the Manor, win back Elise, and give her a life he had previously only dreamed of. He arranged for someone to watch the house for an indefinite time while he was away, not knowing if he would need it again.

"Why don't you buy yourself a fancy carriage to take you on your journey?" Said the man who would take care of the house Garrett had lived in these last several months.

"I couldn't sit in a fancy carriage and dwell on all of my troubles. At least being on horseback keeps my mind in check and gives me something to focus on," he told the man.

"Well, I wish you luck on your trip. I'm sure glad to see this house again. A friend of mine lived here years ago, and I always had fond memories of her. Mary was very kind to every one of us before she died, some fifteen years ago now."

"Mary? Died fifteen years ago?" No, it couldn't be, he thought.

"Aye, a pretty young girl, with long brown hair and a smile for everyone she met. It's too bad what happened to her and her little girl, poor woman lost her life to fever when the child was so young."

Garrett's head was spinning. "The child, do you remember her name?"

"Oh yes, she was a servant girl here until she was taken away. I don't know where she went." Garrett stared at him and he realized he hasn't answered his question. "It was Elise, I believe."

Hearing her name again after all this time, coming to the realization that he had been living in her mother's house, sent chills down his spine. No wonder he felt a sense of comfort in that house, it was where his sweetheart had lived. He suddenly wanted to run to her, to hold her again, and tell her everything that had happened since he left. Out of all the houses he could have lived in, how was it possible that he had picked the house that was so dear to her heart? He knew it was a sign. Of what, he did not know, but he had to find out.

Chapter Fourteen

He traveled for many days, stopping to rest for only a few hours each night, going through freezing rain, bitter cold, and darkness to get to his Elise. Everything he had gone through, months of trying to forget, had vanished. He knew if he could just get to her, just see her glorious face, everything would somehow fall into place.

It occurred to him that she might be married by now, but he still had to see her. He had to tell her that she could be free from her past, and that she could sleep peacefully now. If they weren't married, he would do anything to win her back.

Soon after leaving, he noticed a change was coming over him. He had grown thinner, more tired since he came, and the journey home seemed much harder on him than when he first came. By the time he reached Highfield, every ounce of adrenaline that got him here was gone. He was tired in a way he had never felt before. A sickness had come over him that made his mind unclear. He stopped his horse when he saw the Manor gate. Attempting to dismount, the energy left him and he fell to the ground.

Elise sat in her parlor, reading by the warm hearth. A feeling of dread came over her suddenly, and she turned and looked out the window. Discerning nothing at first, her gaze quickly caught sight of a horse, and instantly her heart began to race. "Raven?" She quickly stood to get a better look and her book fell to the floor. "But where…." Elise saw a body on the ground and her face filled with terror. She ran out to him as fast as she could, fearing the worst.

"Garrett!" Elise shouted. "Stephen! Christina! Come quickly!"

The couple came running out as fast as they could, and saw Elise kneeling down next to Garrett, unconscious and shivering on the ground. "What's happened? Is he hurt?"

She wiped the sweat from his forehead. "He feels very hot. We must get him inside."

Stephen, Jones, and another servant lifted Garrett off the ground. Elise led the way to his room, and Christina sent away for the doctor.

The three of them stood watching over Garrett while they waited for the doctor to arrive. Elise sat by his bedside and held his hand in both of hers. "What's happened to him? Where has he been all this time?"

Stephen stood, arm in arm with his wife, wishing he could somehow help his friend. "He's so pale, he looks like he's been sick for a long time now."

"Heartsick." Christina mentioned. She had met Garrett before, when her family came to pay their respects at the king's funeral. He looked very different now. Weak, almost frail. Like a man who had all but given up on life. Surely, there must be some small measure of hope he was clinging to.

The doctor arrived and Elise stood up to give him room. He examined Garrett while his friends stood in silence. "Hasn't been taking care of himself, has he?" He asked the trio. "Not sleeping, not eating, and traveling like this? It's no wonder he's not awake. Probably exhausted from worry."

Stephen felt so helpless. "What can we do?"

The doctor looked him over several times. "Right now, all we can do is wait. Time will tell. If he wakes, make him rest. He shouldn't be moved at all. Someone should stay with him."

Elise was the first to volunteer. Stephen was quick to follow, but the doctor warned against Christina getting too close.

Elise stayed by his side, day and night. She spoke words of life and love to him, kept his head cool, and watched for any signs of improvement. Stephen relieved her to rest for a few hours each night, but she refused to leave his side any longer than that.

One night, she was scared that he wouldn't wake up. What if he never found out that she was free? They could be together, and everything would be alright, if only he would wake up. There was so much she wanted to say to him, so many questions she wanted to ask. "Garrett, I don't know where you've been or what you've been through. But you're home now and I'm here. I don't want you to leave again. She sat in a rocking chair beside the bed and held his hand, feeling the heat of his fever, watching his chest rise and fall with his short, shallow breaths. "Come back to me, my love."

"Stephen?" His wife called out.

"Yes, dearest?" He loved his new wife more than anything else in the world. The two of them were soulmates. She knew him better than he knew himself.

"There's going to be some changes soon." She looked like she was forming a plan.

He put his arms around her and held her close, breathing in her goodness. "Soon enough, my dear."

She hugged him back and kissed him softly. "I mean, with Garrett being home again. I know you spent weeks searching for him when he left, and I know that you felt like it was your fault that he left in the first place."

He turned his head away from her and gave a long, weary sigh. "It was my fault; it may have been a misunderstanding, and with the best of intentions, but my doing, none the less."

She stood beside him and took his hand. "It may have started out that way, but now you have a chance to make it right. Forgive yourself. Welcome your friend back, for good."

"I'm not sure how. What if I mess everything up again?" His voice started to break. "What if it's too late, and Garrett doesn't recover from this? The last time I ever spoke to him, I told him to leave." He started to shake as he fought back the tears. "I might never get the chance to make this right, to be his friend."

She comforted him and wisely let him work through the things he was feeling, knowing he had kept these things in for far too long. "You have to hope, Stephen. Hold on to the hope that you will get that chance, and that you can make this right by your friend, as well as your sister, by making plans for them and their future."

She told him about the conversation she'd had with Hazel and helped him understand why he was feeling like this. A new understanding came over Stephen, everything he was going through making more sense now.

"Please tell me how to make this right, I need your help. I need your guidance." Stephen's voice had taken on a desperation that his wife had not heard before.

"We will figure it out together." She kissed him and held him for a long time, then said goodnight, knowing he wouldn't be able to sleep while his friend was in this condition.

Hours later, in the dead of night, the Manor was very quiet. Stephen walked the halls, fearfully waiting, too anxious for the health of his friend to try to sleep. What a mess he had made of things. He paced and worried, back and forth.

Garrett woke up in a fog. Wiping the sleep from his eyes, he felt disoriented. His mind was racing with distorted memories. The last night that he spent here, knowing his love was going to be taken away from him by a man he thought was his friend. The angry and obsessive thoughts that kept him awake at night while he was away. Chasing the demons of another while in turn, forming his own. Feverish and confused, he looked around the room, trying to fix his eyes on something that would bring his mind into focus.

He saw Elise, quietly sleeping in a chair by his side. Her hair was laying softly around her shoulders, her hands lying gracefully in her lap. The memory of the first day they met came flooding to the surface, and he remembered being the one by her bedside while she slept. Garrett tried to remember the feeling of catching her, when suddenly, a new image clouded his memory. Instead of feeling her safely in his arms, he saw Stephen pushing him away to catch her instead. He laughed at Garrett before carrying her away. The false memory and delirium fueled his misplaced anger, and gave him the focus that he was searching for when deciding on his next move.

He got up slowly, confused with fever and disoriented by weakness. A strength that must have come from pure adrenaline now flowed through him. He made his way out without waking her and began walking toward the prince's study. He had to stop him. Had to tell him now, while he still could. His mind saw nothing but his anger. No matter what happened, at least he would know that he tried. He stopped suddenly when he saw Stephen in the hallway.

"Garrett, my friend! Are you well?" Stephen was happy to see him up but saw immediately in his face that something was very wrong. He looked like a wild animal, his eyes shifting and unfocused. A sudden and eerie fear crept over Stephen face.

Unsteady on his feet and full of so many emotions; rage, defeat, bitterness, it all came flying out. "YOU!" He pointed at Stephen, all but snarling his words. "You took her away from me!"

Stephen was shocked and scared at this change in his friend. "Please, let me help you back to your room, the fever…"

"No! You took her away from me, you want to keep her for yourself! You drove me away so you could keep us apart!"

"Garrett, please, my friend, you don't understand…"

Suddenly a fist swung at him and he landed on the ground, his jaw throbbing. "Garrett, stop, it's me! I'm your friend!"

"Friend?! A friend would push me away, shut me out, and take from me everything I held dear?!" His eyes plainly showed his delusion. The fever was twisting his mind.

Servants rushed over to them to help and Stephen put his hands up to stop them. "No, stay back, let me talk to him, he isn't himself."

Elise had woken up to find him gone, then came out of the room and ran to Stephen. "Please, you have to tell him, now before we lose him entirely." She looked into Garrett's eyes. "He's going mad."

Garrett looked so lost, confused, and hurt. Knowing the day would come when he would stand up to the prince for taking away his love was the only thing that had kept him going in his journey, and he was going to have it out, even if it took his very life.

Stephen nodded his head at Elise and, breathing heavily, tried to control the situation and get his friend back to reality. "Garrett, listen to me, please, just listen. I didn't tell you the truth when Elise came here, and then you misunderstood what was going on." He spoke slowly, his voice full of uncertainty. "I didn't bring her here to marry her, nor was that ever my intention." He stretched out a hand in his direction. "If anything, I brought her here for you."

Garrett's face was full of anger. His legs shook with weakness and his whole body ached. He could feel that he was near the end, and this was the one and only thing that mattered anymore. He raised his fist again.

"Wait!" Stephen pleaded. "She's my sister."

Anger turned into confusion. Already disoriented with fever, he didn't understand what was being said. "What? What did you say?"

There was a long pause. He grew very pale and they could see that he didn't have much time. Elise spoke, calmly and gently. "Garrett? Did you hear what he said?"

He turned to her, and she saw the desperation in his eyes. "I'm sorry," he whispered. He then turned toward Stephen, with every ounce of rage that he could summon, took out a knife that had appeared in his hand, and stabbed him.

Elise screamed as Garrett dropped the knife and fell to his knees.

Garrett tried to sort out what had just happened in his twisted and clouded mind. He looked down at his blood covered hands, unknown to him now, and then up at his friend. "What have I done?"

A spark of maddened energy came over him, he looked around at his friends in horror, picked himself up off the ground, and ran out the front door.

Elise started to run after him, but Christina stopped her. She had been watching the ordeal from her bedroom door, tucked away from danger. "No, Elise, let him go."

She turned into her sister's arms, put her head down on Christina's shoulder, and wept over what she had witnessed. After some time had passed and they had processed what happened, she called for Jones and ordered him to bring Garrett back.

Jones grabbed a lantern, asked a guard to accompany him, and went out the front door, assuming Garrett would be hiding in the stables.

Upon reaching the stables, they approached cautiously, not wanting to spook Garrett in his current mental state. Jones held the lantern high as they quietly peered into each stall, gently speaking words of calm, hoping to lure him out of hiding.

"It's alright, sir, come out and we can talk about this, don't be afraid." They reached the stall where Raven was kept, but were confused to see the gate open and the stall empty.

"Jones, when did you last see Garrett's horse?" One of the guards asked.

He shook his head. "She was here when I fed them tonight. You don't think he…"

The guard closed his eyes and sighed heavily. "That's exactly what I think."

Garrett rode deliriously into town. "What have I done? Oh, what have I done?!" He had done the worst possible thing, something he didn't even think he was capable of, something he didn't want to be capable of. His clouded judgement and horrified mind could think of only one place he could hide. Arriving at the edge of the village, he turned his horse around, told her to go home, and set her off in the direction of the Manor. Not wanting to be seen, he headed toward Jane's house under the cover of the night sky. Slipping cautiously into her side garden, Garrett made his way to the back of the house and knocked softly on the door.

He waited for what seemed like an eternity and knocked again, louder. Peering over his shoulder to make sure he wasn't seen, he raised his arm to knock a third time. "Jane?" he whispered.

The door opened slowly and Jane lifted a tired face to see who it was, thinking someone from the village was sending for a midwife. She was surprised at first to see her friend standing there, then her expression turned to shock when she saw his altered state. "Garrett? Is that you? What's wrong?"

He quickly made his way inside, looking ominous. "I've done something terrible, Jane, please you have to help me!" He began to cough painfully, she locked the door and gestured to a chair for him to rest in.

"Of course, I'll be right back." Jane hurried to her bedroom door. She woke her husband and told him to come and help, not knowing what scrape her friend had gotten into.

"I didn't even know he was back here, did he tell you where he's been?" Henry hurriedly dressed and followed his wife out to where she had left Garrett.

"No, he hasn't told me anything, but I think something is very wrong."

They quickly reached him, he was shivering in the chair and mumbling something under his breath. Henry looked at Jane, his eyes wide with shock. "I told you" she affirmed.

Henry instructed his wife to fetch a blanket to wrap around his shoulders. He touched his hot and clammy forehead and tried to speak to him. "Garrett? Can you hear me?"

Garrett seemed un-phased by their presence, his fever taking an even greater hold over his mind. "I didn't mean to, I'm sorry, I'm so sorry! Don't let them find me!"

"It's alright, now, no one is coming to get you, and you're safe now." Jane tried to reason with him. What had her friend so deathly scared?

By this point, Garrett was shaking violently, his breath became shallow and labored. "You don't understand, you don't know what I've done."

"What is it, what is this thing you've done?"

His eyes began to glaze over, as if he was somewhere else. He tried to make sense of the images in his mind. He saw himself back at Highfield, at that final moment when he was on his knees and looking at his hands. In his manic state, he saw his hands covered in blood. "I've killed Prince Stephen."

With that horrified admission, they saw the lights go out in his eyes, and he passed out, dropping fully into the chair.

Jane looked at her husband, "What should we do?"

He shook his head. "Come on, let's get him into a room."

They got him to his feet and had to practically drag him into a spare bedroom. They kept this room at the ready for times when people needed very close care. Henry got him into the bed while his wife brought the things they would need to help him.

"Should we call for the doctor?" she asked her husband.

"No, not yet. If what he says is true, then we don't have a leader. It could start a war. I've seen people in this state before, let's keep him here and do what we can for him, at least it will buy us some time to try to sort things out."

Chapter Fifteen

A few week passed, with no news of Garrett. They had stayed at the Manor all this time, fearing to leave even for a day, thinking he would return. Elise didn't know what to make of things. She sat with Christina in the parlor.

"Where do you think he went?" She asked sheepishly.

Her sister looked into the fireplace, "Back to where he was before, I suppose."

She looked down at the ground, trying to make sense of everything that had happened. "He didn't seem well enough to leave."

"Well enough, apparently." She was angry at Garrett for what he had done to her husband.

Elise felt a tear run down her cheek. "I thought….I thought when Stephen told him I was his sister, everything would be alright."

Christina held her hand out to her in a gesture of support, and she took it, grateful for her presence. "I did too. I think he's hiding somewhere, processing everything that happened, or he could be ashamed of his actions and too fearful to make himself known. We need to wait and see."

Elise nodded at the wise words of her sister. She didn't want to feel like Garrett had permanently turned into the person he was that night. All she could do was wait.

"While we wait," Christina looked at her sister. "It might be helpful to have some good news?"

Elise looked puzzled for a moment before her eyes lit up with joy. She knew Christina had her suspicions, but now she were sure. A new little prince or princess was on the way.

"You are looking better today, how do you feel?" Jane had worked tirelessly with her husband to restore the health of her friend. His fever had broken a few days after he came to them, and today he was able to sit up in the bed, color starting to come back to his face. They knew he still had a long way to go, but he was mending well in the care of his friends.

Garrett smiled weakly at her, grateful to have a safe haven. "I am feeling better, thanks to you and Henry." His face clouded over with grief as he remembered that each day he was here, his friends were in danger, knowing it was only a matter of time before the royal guards found him. What would they do to Jane and Henry for their concealment of him? He had to get his strength back, so he could leave before anything happened.

Jane finished checking on him, then left him to rest. She closed the door and went to speak to her husband in the adjoining room.

"Have you heard anything from town?" she asked.

Henry shook his head. "Nothing, not a word of it. I don't know what to make of it all, and I don't want to ask questions in fear of raising suspicions."

She nodded her head. "I know. If we even try to find out what happened, we could cause even more harm. How can he be sure of what happened that night? He was out of his mind."

"Have the children found out he is here?" he asked.

"No, they think we are caring for an elderly man."

He nodded his head. "Just as well, best to keep them out of it."

Another week passed and Garrett was now strong enough to consider his next step. A shadow of his former self, he was still very weak. He stayed in his room each day while the children were awake and then joined the adults in the evenings, making sure to stay safely hidden. One night, he went to them for advice.

"I've had a lot of time to think about this, and I've decided to turn myself in."

"No Garrett, you can't be serious." Jane tried to talk her friend out of this crazy idea.

He was adamant. "I want to be held accountable for what I've done."

Henry interjected. "She's right, Garrett, you can't do that. There is a reason no one else knows. Elise must be keeping it a secret until she can figure out what to do. If they weren't married yet then it means there is no royal family left."

"They must have been married. Stephen sent us a letter saying he wanted to be married right away, and that was months ago." Garrett felt sick saying the words.

"But wouldn't we have known if a wedding had taken place?" Jane asked.

Garrett pondered this. "Elise would have only agreed to a private, small wedding. They probably didn't even have a ceremony."

Henry interrupted his thoughts. "Either way, if the prince is dead and no one knows, you need to leave, for the safety of our country. Come into town with us tomorrow, we will take the carriage so no one sees you. We can get what you will need before you leave."

Garrett agreed and they made plans for the next day.

"Let's go into town today," Christina asked her sister, "I want to get some yarn for a blanket. My mother made a blanket for each of her children before they were born, and I want to carry on the tradition."

Elise had put her grief to the side to share this special time with her sister. A baby would bring so much needed joy to the family. "I would love to go into town with you, can we stop and see Grace, as well?"

Christina had been introduced to Grace the first time they went into town together, and the ladies had become fast friends. "Of course."

They ordered the carriage and an escort, and then said goodbye to Hazel. She was given instructions on what to do if Garrett came back.

A scenic ride brought them to the village center. Christina had become unwell and asked that Elise go on without her, and she would catch up. Elise left her in the care of her escort and walked on, allowing her sister some privacy. The flower shop caught her eye and she made her way to it, giving herself a moment to think about her love.

Garrett couldn't believe it. Sitting here in Jane and Henry's carriage, concealed from everyone in town while they gathered supplies, he thought he must be seeing a vision. He watched as Elise walked alone into the flower shop. She looked happy, glowing even. She wasn't dressed in black.

"They must not have gotten married." He thought to himself, feeling desire and passion for the first time in months. So Elise didn't marry Stephen, after all. His heart began to beat faster. But that would mean Henry was right, and the country was left without a leader. He knew he had to leave before anyone found out, but maybe he could see her one last time…..

He slipped quietly out of the carriage, careful that no one could see him, and ran back behind the flower shop, watching her through the window. He felt his cheeks flush at the sight of her. "Elise" he whispered to the wind.

She walked around, smelling the various flowers, thinking about her first visit here, and wishing more than anything that she would see Garrett again someday. No matter what had happened or how much time had passed, she still had so much love in her heart for him.

Garrett turned quickly out of view and went to the back door of the shop. He had to see her, one last time. He knew it was risky, and he didn't know what she would do, but he had to try, before it was too late. If he could just see her once more, hold her in his arms one final time, he could leave. He quietly opened the door just enough to see inside and waited for her to come close.

Elise started to hum, lost in thought. She was daydreaming about the last night they had spent together, and could almost feel him close to her again, almost smell his scent. She walked closer and closer to the back of the shop, when suddenly the door opened and a hand grabbed onto her.

She began to gasp until she looked up and saw who it was. Her pulse began to race, and she opened her mouth to say his name when he quickly put a finger over his lips to beg for silence. She nodded and walked out the door with him, looking over her shoulder to make sure no one saw.

"You're here!" she exclaimed with hushed tones. She was so happy to see him again, he looked so much better than he had that night. "Where have you been? I've been so worried…."

Garrett couldn't take it any longer. He wrapped his arms around her waist, pulled her tight against him, and kissed her passionately. She could feel the warmth of his body next to hers while she kissed him back, not caring about anything else. Right here, in this moment, all was right in the world.

He pulled back from the embrace, both of them out of breath.

"I'm so sorry, Elise, what you must think of me….please forgive me, I didn't mean…"

Garrett looked so altered that Elise didn't know how to react. All this time, she thought he was so far away, and he was right here.

"I just had to see you again." Garrett took a few steps back before turning and running away.

"Garrett, wait!" She cried.

Just as quickly as he appeared, he was gone again.

Elise ran back to the carriage to find Christina just getting out. She saw her sister coming and started to wave her off.

"I'm fine, I'm fine, just needed a moment, truly."

Elise grabbed her sister's hands and gave her a serious look. "I've just seen Garrett." She whispered.

They quickly climbed back into the carriage and closed the door. She told him how scared he looked and what he said, and that he was trying to stay out of sight.

Christina considered her words and tried to make sense of his actions. "Let's go and talk to Jane and Grace, maybe they know something."

Their first stop was Jane's house, but no one was home. This didn't surprise them, due to the nature of their work. They went instead to Grace's house, and were graciously welcomed. They sat for a while, drinking tea and asking all the proper questions, but Grace could tell they were distracted. She urged them to speak openly to her.

"Do you remember my friend Garrett?" she asked.

Grace nodded. "Of course, from the first time you came."

"Have you seen him….recently?" Christina asked, afraid to reveal too much.

There was a moment of hesitation, "Well, actually…"

"Please," Elise urged. "Anything you can tell us will help."

Grace set her cup down. She seemed to be choosing her words carefully. "I thought I was seeing things. A couple of weeks ago, the baby was up to nurse. I sat with her at the window and looked out into the night sky. I saw what I thought must have been a shadow, but when I looked closer I saw it was a man. I almost sent for the police, thinking it was a thief, but it was Garrett, I'm sure of it. Only, he was acting so strange, sneaking around, hunched over. It was like he was out of his mind. I didn't know what to make of it."

Elise was on the edge of her seat listening to her friend's account.

Christina advised her sister to return to the Manor with her so they could come up with a plan. They thanked Grace, said goodbye to the children, and made their way back to the carriage.

Elise turned and looked around before getting inside. She felt a sick feeling in her gut at the thought of leaving him the way things were. What if she never saw him again?

"We will find him." Christina assured her.

She nodded her head and made herself step into the carriage.

Christina had her reasons for wanting to find him. Thinking of what Garrett had done to her husband, she wanted to confront him. Even though she knew her sister still had feelings for him, she wanted him face the consequences.

Jane and Henry were mortified when they finished their shopping and came back to an empty carriage, but were relieved when they found Garrett back at the house. "We thought they had taken you."

"I'm sorry, I…had to take care of some things. Henry, I understand now why I must go, I'm ready."

Jane looked at her husband. "How long can your sister keep the children today?"

He nodded his head at her. "I'll go over and ask for them to stay the night, she won't mind."

She sent him on his way and told him to get back as quickly as possible, then she turned her attention to Garrett. She showed him the various things they had gathered in town; bedding, a canteen for water, food for several days, a rope and small hatchet. Arranging them all on a table, she produced a bag to carry everything, and then helped him pack.

"Someday, when I get my affairs in order, I'll pay you back." He assured her. He had accidentally left the papers for his Uncle's fortune in Raven's pack before sending her back to the Manor.

By now, Henry had returned. "None of that talk, you don't owe us a single thing. We take care of our friends."

"Even if they are in trouble?" He questioned.

Jane interjected. "Especially when they are in trouble."

They finished packing everything he would need, fed him a hot meal, and prepared for him to leave. Henry gave him his cloak to offer concealment, and offered to take him as far as he could on foot. Knowing he still wasn't fully mended, he accepted the offer graciously, knowing he would need any help he could get if he was to survive.

Jane heard a commotion outside and peered out the window to see what was going on. She spotted several royal guards on horseback.

"Henry! Get him out! The back door, quickly!"

He sprinted to the window to see what she meant. "Royal guards! They are coming for you, we must leave now!"

They quickly gathered their things before rushing to the back door, afraid to lose even a moment of time. Garrett's face was full of fear, regret, and hopelessness, his heart racing and his mind working fast.

As Jane watched the guards out the window, she saw the royal carriage turn the corner and stop in front of her door. She said a quick prayer and opened her door, ready to lie about her friend's whereabouts, when the carriage door opened and she gasped. "Henry! Come back! Henry!!"

She left her door open and ran to the back door, finding them with a puzzled look. "What are you doing?! You will lead them right to us!" Henry whispered.

Jane took Garrett's hand and pulled him toward the front room with haste. "Come quickly!"

Garrett followed her to the front room, not knowing what awaited him there. He imagined the guards had paid her or threatened her to give him up. He braced himself, only to enter the room and see what he thought must be a ghost. His face turned white and his heart nearly stopped in shock.

"S..Stephen? Is that you?"

The prince stood before him, wringing his hands in desperation. "Look, Garrett, I don't know what it is you're hiding from, but you need to stop this foolishness and come home."

Garrett looked as though he might faint. He looked down at his hands and pictured them covered in Stephen's blood. "I don't understand. I….I killed you."

Stephen let out a nervous laugh. "Killed me? What? I admit, you can throw quite a punch, even when you're half dead. I couldn't smile for days," he put his hand up to cradle his jaw, remembering the pain. "But you didn't get to do anything else before you ran off."

Garrett's knees wobbled and his head became cloudy, Stephen and Henry had to move quickly to catch him.

"Easy now, help me get him onto the chair."

Garrett sat down and put his head in his hands, steadying his thoughts. "I don't understand."

The four sat down and tried to piece together what had happened. In Garrett's mind, he remembered arriving at Highfield, being angry, and then seeing the knife and the blood all over his hands. That was all he remembered. Stephen gently recalled the actual events. He punched him, they tried to reason with him, and then he ran away. Garrett was shocked. Once he wrapped his mind around the fact that he had not murdered his best friend, he was much more open to the truth.

"I was at the Manor for days?" He asked, not believing he both acted out of delirium and had also lost time. The story Stephen told was completely different from what his maddened mind lead him to believe. He was so relieved.

"I knew something was off when you got up, you should have seen your face when I told you Elise was my sister."

"Your what!?" Henry, Jane, and Garrett all shouted at once.

Stephen's face broke into a smile. "You really don't remember any of it, do you?"

He retold them all the story from the beginning. His father's letter, his fears about Garrett leaving, finding hope in Elise, and his marriage to Christina. Garrett tried to wrap his head around it all.

"Now that you know the truth, will you come back home?" He asked, hopeful.

Garrett had tears in his eyes from taking everything in. "Are you sure you want me back?"

Stephen put his hand on his friends shoulder. "You belong with us, with your family."

The two friends shared a tearful and forgiving embrace, then Stephen let out a long sigh of relief. "Let's go home."

They gathered all of Garrett's things into the carriage, thanked Henry and Jane for their kindness, and climbed inside.

As the carriage made its way out of Westmore toward Highfield, Garrett wanted to confess to his friend. "There's something I need to tell you, before we get there."

"Please" Stephen urged, "anything you need."

"I think I know why, in the delirium, I thought I wanted to kill you."

Stephen raised his eyebrow in anticipation.

"Don't tell Elise this, but I went to confront the man that she was with before. By the time I got there, and saw with my own eyes the harm he was doing, Stephen I wanted to kill him. Fortunately, I was spared from doing anything like that, but it stayed with me, the anger I felt." Garrett waited for his response.

"So the unresolved anger for him turned into misguided anger toward me?"

Garrett nodded his head, hoping he was making sense.

"I see what you mean. Honestly if you could have seen yourself, you really were out of your mind, and very confused. It must have been like having a nightmare."

Garrett nodded again and Stephen smiled. "It's all over now."

The rest of the ride home was quiet, as Garrett soon fell asleep. Stephen could tell that while the sickness had left him, it had taken a toll on him, and he was still very frail. He vowed to help his friend return to his full strength, hoping he wouldn't succumb to the same fate his father had. He allowed him to rest peacefully until they reached the gate of Highfield Manor, then he gently woke him up. Garrett jumped, startled. "Its's alright now, my friend. We're home."

"I don't know what to say to her." He admitted, suddenly feeling quite shy.

Stephen laughed. "I don't think you will have the chance to say anything." He winked at his friend.

The ladies were waiting impatiently at the door, hoping for good news. Christina held Elise's trembling hands in her own, both of them hoping Garrett was found safe. The carriage stopped and Stephen got out, smiling broadly. He nodded his head at Elise and beckoned her to approach the carriage. She ran to it and quickly climbed inside.

Christina waited for her husband. "What is it? Have you found him?"

He wrapped his arms around her. "I told you I would bring him home, didn't I?" He leaned down and kissed his wife. "Let's go inside and let them have some privacy."

"Not until I hear he has apologized for hitting you." Christina wanted that for him.

Stephen laughed. "He did." He assured her. "But, once you hear what he thought happened, I don't think you will mind so much."

As Stephen predicted, Garrett didn't have time to utter a single word before his beloved enveloped him in her arms and kissed him passionately. The time that had passed had changed them both, but had only deepened their love for each other. They stopped to catch their breath, holding each other close. He placed his forehead on hers, and breathed her in.

"Don't ever leave me again, Garrett. If you come back, you come back to stay. Promise me."

A single tear escaped his eye as he whispered back, "I promise".

Chapter Sixteen

As the days and weeks passed, Garrett's strength slowly returned. He got to know Stephens wife, and they became fast friends. Christina forgave the punch he had given her husband once she understood the delirium he had that night. Spring came to the countryside, and Garrett was soon strong enough to walk outdoors, with Elise at his side. He had been back home for several weeks, and was quickly recovering.

Sitting in the main parlor one night, the men listened to the ladies talk about the new baby, who would be arriving within the next few months. Christina had almost everything ready, and couldn't wait to meet their child.

"So what about you?" Stephen asked Garrett, quietly. "The baby will need an uncle, you know."

Garrett colored warmly, then looked across the room at Elise.

"Do you think she would still marry me?" He asked seriously.

Stephen nodded his head at his friend. "I know she would. I know she's been dreaming about it ever since the night you two spent in that patch of forest you went to."

Garrett looked up at his friend. "She told you about that?"

He smiled and nodded. "She told me a lot of things while you were gone." He winked and suddenly Garrett remembered the nights they spent together, seemingly innocent, but still with the intentions of two people in love.

"I'm not sure I can be what she needs me to be. She needs someone strong, who can keep her safe…" His voice trailed off and he thought of the promise he made her months ago. He left to slay her demons and had returned a haunted man.

"This isn't going to last forever, you almost lost your life. It's going to take some time to recover from that, but you will recover, I guarantee it." He had so much faith in him.

"How do you know? How do you know if I can be the man I once was?" He questioned.

He motioned to Elise. "Look at her. Don't you remember how scared and shy she was when she first came here?"

Garrett watched her, laughing and talking openly with Christina. No, she was not the same girl who came to them a year ago. Now she was full of life and spirit, she was graceful and confidant.

Stephen disturbed his thought. "She was hurting once, too. You were there for her when no one else was. Now she has the chance to return the favor. Broken people can heal, Garrett."

The prince stood to his feet. "Take all the time you need, my friend, but think about it." Stephen patted him on the back, then went to join his wife and sister.

"I will" Garrett whispered to himself. He felt something stir inside of him, from a place he thought the sickness had taken forever. It was a fire that burned with the determination to rise again. "I will beat this." He said to himself.

Will Stephens help, and the constant encouragement from the ladies, Garrett began to rebuild his strength. Short walks around the Manor turned into long trips around the grounds, and visits to his stables soon became gentle horseback riding. Raven seemed to sense the need to go slowly, happy to go out and explore again. In the evenings, he would use his woodworking tools while he rested, gaining strength back in his hands.

Within weeks, everyone seemed completely at home with each other. Stephen was so in love with his wife, and so anxious for the birth of his child. He planned his official coronation a few months after the baby would be born, and then his little family would move into the castle. He watched Garrett and Elise carefully, anxious to have them married before they left. He hadn't told them yet, but his gift to them upon news of their engagement would be the Manor they had all been living in over the last year. It was Christina's idea and it was perfect. He wanted to tell them soon, but he knew Garrett wanted to wait to propose until he felt like himself again.

On a warm sunny day towards the end of spring, Jane came to visit with the ladies and Garrett asked his friend for some help. They worked together all afternoon on his project and finished up just in time as Jane left to go home. She winked at the gentleman as she was leaving, knowing she was meant to be a distraction. Stephen gave Garrett a nod of approval and he walked up to Elise. "Will you go with me somewhere?"

Elise looked lovingly at him, so happy to see he had regained his full health and strength. "Anywhere."

He walked her out to the stables and secured two horses. They rode side by side into the forest, and then he turned toward the familiar path they once took. Carefully, they made their way to the clearing, but this time, there was a surprise.

A blanket was set up in the middle, by the stream, with flowers and candles placed all around. "What's all this?" She asked, delighted.

"It's time I told you something," he lead her over to the blanket and sat down beside her. "Elise, when I left here, months ago, I went to Mournstead."

She was equal parts horrified and puzzled. Why would anyone go there, knowing what she went through?

"Back when I thought you were intended for Stephen, I felt like I was still connected to you, and that I had to protect you from things he couldn't. I bought a house there and went to confront Mr. Devlin."

She shuddered at the mention of his name, and felt her heart race at the thought of her perfect love, standing in the very house of the man who had threatened and beaten her.

"Elise, when I got there, he had been dead for some time. They think he drank himself to death."

She felt sick to her stomach, but at the same time, a sense of relief.

"He won't ever hurt you or anyone else again." He promised. She closed her eyes and laid her head down on his shoulder.

"When you went to his home, was there…..was there another servant?"

Garrett had waited until this moment to tell her about Clara. He wanted to wait for the right time, as not to further traumatize her. "Yes, he had acquired another young servant girl, around 15 years old, sometime after you left him. Her name is Clara, she was with him for several months, and…"

He paused, unsure of how she would take his next words, "....she was pregnant, with Mr. Devlin's child."

"Oh no, oh I can't believe..." Elise tried to sort out the information he had given her. "What happened to her?"

As he unfolded the events during the time he had spent in Mournstead, she listened with awe. He told her about Florence, the time they spent together, and about the house he had purchased for them. She was engrossed in his story with tear filled eyes, feeling both horrified at the things she knew Clara must have endured, and passionate in her desire to help her heal from them.

"Thank you, Garrett. Thank you for everything you did for her, for all of them. I know some of what she must have gone through, but I can't even imagine the rest."

He looked across the meadow for a time, lost in his memories. "I just wanted to help her, somehow. I wanted to help her find some semblance of happiness after the terrible things she had endured. I wanted something beautiful in its place, a happy, loving home."

He took a folded up letter from his jacket pocket, opened it, and handed it to Elise. "Jane received this today and brought it to me when she first came in." It was a letter from Florence, announcing the birth of her grandson, baby Christopher. Clara had fallen completely in love with him, forgetting the past in the gift of this beautiful new future. Mother and baby were doing well, and they asked for a visit from him soon.

Elise read the letter with a sense of peace. Garrett had gone to the darkest part of her past, had rescued someone from a fate she had fought so long against, and had restored a life that would have been tragically lost.

"There's more I need to tell you. I went to the town leaders and arranged for the house to be burned down. They allowed me to choose what I wanted done with the land, and I knew it wasn't enough just to erase the evil that had been done, I had to put something in its place that would restore goodness. We built a children's home, and dozens of rose bushes were planted around it as a memorial to all the servants who had been hurt or killed, and a reminder that it will no longer be tolerated."

He then told her about Mournstead becoming part of Glendale, so that the small village would now be held accountable by the legislation of the larger town. Then he told her about her mother's home, how shocked he was to find out it was hers, and the unexpected sense of peace he felt while living in it.

Her tears were so many, they now flowed freely. He did this for her. This wonderful, amazing thing. He left his home and his dreams to do this for a woman he thought he couldn't have. What selfless love.

"Garrett, why did you go to such lengths to do all of this?" She asked.

"Because I vowed once to protect you. When I knew I couldn't be near you, I had to find another way. I wanted to protect you from your nightmares by taking away the reasons for them."

She was amazed, and overwhelmed. How could someone love her as much as Garrett loved her? How could her heart hold any more joy than it already did?

"Elise, now that we can be together, and I've protected you from your past, will you trust me to protect you in our future?" He opened up a small box that held an ornate ring, it was a delicate circle of tiny, golden roses. "Will you marry me?"

Overcome with emotion and unable to speak, she nodded softly, smiled brightly, and then held out her hand. Garrett slipped the ring onto her finger, and he felt the weight he had carried for over a year fall away, knowing it was all worth it.

"Garrett," she whispered, "promise me that there won't ever be anymore secrets between us, from now on."

He knew he could tell her now about his recent fortune. He hadn't told anyone yet, not even Stephen. "There is something else, then, that you need to know." He began. "I poured everything I had into your village. I thought I was alone in the world and that it didn't matter anymore, so I spent everything."

Elise shook her head at him. "Don't you know that I don't care about that? I just want to be with you, nothing else matters!" Thinking the conversation was over, she went back to kissing him, but he stopped her.

"No, that's not what I…..as much as I appreciate…"

"Stephen, won't you tell me where they went? It's been hours! Garrett hasn't even left the Manor grounds since he came back!"

"But he has, my dear." Stephen teased his wife mercilessly.

Christina tried to think of a time in the last 2 months that Garrett had left the grounds. "Dear, I know he hasn't left, not these last several months!"

"He has left the grounds. Earlier today while you and Elise were visiting with Jane." He had Garrett's blessing to tell Christina what was going on, but this was much more fun.

"Today? Now I know you two are up to something. He wasn't in the village, was he?" She tried to squeeze an explanation out of her husband.

"No, he wasn't in the village." He was trying very hard not to laugh.

"Stephen, you tell me right this instant where those two went!" She was growing impatient with sheer excitement.

"Oh all right, since you asked so nicely." She gave him a sideways look at his childish ways, and he grinned at her before he continued. He told her what Garrett had said to him earlier, about his time away from them and what he had accomplished in Mournstead. She knew he was a good man, but this was above and beyond what any man would willingly do for a woman he couldn't even have.

Stephen was beaming. "Garrett is like a brother to me, and now, he truly will be my brother. A little over a year ago I had no one. My father was gone, my best friend was planning to leave, and I faced a very lonely future. How could I lead a kingdom if I had no one to support me through it?"

She wrapped her arms around him. "Now you have an entire family who loves you."

He held her as tight as her growing belly would allow. "Now I have a sister, a wife, a child on the way, and soon, a brother." He paused. "That is, if Elise says yes."

She laughed at the idea. "I think it's safe to say she will."

While the sun was setting, Stephen and Christina tried their best to wait patiently to greet the newly affianced couple. They finally appeared and it was all Christina could do to keep calm and still. Eventually, they did come in to share their news, and they were all so overjoyed.

Chapter Seventeen

The evenings became longer now with spring in full bloom. Christina spent many of them in Elise's parlor while she waited for the birth of her first child. The sisters were each other's confidant, and trusted ally.

"Have you and Garrett talked about how many children you will have?" Christina was still knitting that tiny blanket she started months ago, hoping to finish it in time.

Elise was sipping tea and looking down at her ring, glistening in the light of the setting sun. "We are hoping for at least two."

"One of each, then?" Christina put the blanket down just long enough to pick up her tea and take a sip. "That's how it is in my family. My brother is much older than me, though. I hope mine are closer in age." She picked the blanket back up, determined.

"I don't mind if they are a few years apart, but you're right, I do want them fairly close. I bet Stephan wants a dozen," she said, laughing.

Christina shot her an incredulous look. "A dozen! Oh no, I couldn't possibly keep track of so many! Four or five, more likely." She tied off the last stitch and proudly held the blanket up for display. "There! It's ready!"

Elise reached out to feel the blanket and marveled at its silkiness. "How lovely! What joy to have something so precious to wrap him in! Or, she, I suppose."

Christina folded it carefully across her swollen belly. "Oh It's a 'he' I'm sure." She took her friends hand and placed it over her stomach to feel the baby move. "I don't think a girl would kick me so hard!"

Elise laughed and marveled at the feel of the baby. She wondered what it would be like with her own baby in time.

"I remember the births of several babies from my village. The midwife even let me help a few times."

Christina's eyes grew wide. "Really? That must have been thrilling!"

Elise nodded her head, her eyes unfocused, remembering. "It was. Seeing new life being brought into the world! While we waited, she would tell me so many stories of the different births she had witnessed. I especially likes the stories of difficult births and how she always knew what to do to overcome those challenges to allow the baby to be born. I don't know that I would be so fearless in that kind of situation."

She paused, and Christina put her hand over her shoulder. She had every confidence in her sister's abilities. "Elise, knowing this about you, I would feel safer if you would come and be with me when its time. Will you?"

Her eyes shone with love at her sister's kind request. "Of course I will."

The next day, Elise asked Garrett to request a visit from Jane and Henry. She wanted to see her friends again, but that was not the reason for this trip. She sought after Jane's advice about the upcoming birth. Henry would supply her with elixirs and medicinal teas like she had seen in her past experiences, and Jane would tell her some things to watch for. Maybe she would feel better if she was more prepared.

Jane and her family joyfully accepted the request, and came the very next day. The twins were so happy to see Garrett again, and he marveled at how much they had grown.

"Probably too old for toys, now that you are almost 8?" He hoped they weren't quite too old yet, as he did have one final surprise for them.

"Well," Alexander began. "We are very old now….."

His twin sister Amelia rolled her eyes at him, "You might be too old, but I'm not! Do you have another horse for me, Uncle Garrett?"

Garrett stood up and took on a sorrowful expression. "No, I'm sorry, I haven't made any more horses."

Amelia dropped her shoulders in defeat, and he saw Alexander show the tiniest bit of disappointment.

"However," he began, this time in a joyful tone, "We did make something…..for…..the horses."

The twins looked at each other, eyes wide. "For the horses?"

Garrett and Elise went to a low table and pulled off the cover that concealed the most intricate work he had ever done. It was a wooden playset comprised of a small farmhouse and a set of stables. Elise and Garrett had made it together, Garrett creating the structure, and Elise preparing items for the inside. It had been an excellent way to rebuild his strength. The house had little beds, tables and chairs, even curtains, all sewed with her loving hands. The stables had bales of hay, feeding troughs, and even tiny brushes.

The children gasped in delight and ran to the gift. "Thank you Uncle Garrett, thank you Aunt Elise!"

The ladies clapped their hands in approval and Henry shook Garrett's hand. "What a masterpiece, my friend, and who better to craft it?"

"Thank you, Henry, it was truly a pleasure, for both of us."

With the children playing, Jane motioned for Elise to meet her in the adjoining room, so that they could speak privately. She had several books and illustrations with her.

"I don't wish to scare Christina, but there are a few things you will need to know just in case I'm not here when the time comes, or if there is a delay in my arrival. Sometimes babies are early, or late. Sometimes they come right out without help, and sometimes you need to act very quickly."

Elise felt sure that Christina would labor long enough to get Jane there in time, but she was grateful for the impromptu lesson. Jane explained the basics to her, and told her how to spot many possible complications and what to do. Elise had several questions that Jane answered the best she could. "Don't worry. If something happens and I'm not there, you will know what to do." She assured her with a confident smile.

She then went to examine Christina as she had several times during her pregnancy. Elise joined her and Jane explained everything she was looking for, how well the baby was growing, and what to expect in the coming weeks. "You are young and strong and healthy, and I expect everything to go smoothly," were her parting words of assurance.

Later that night, Elise and Garrett shared a blanket out on his balcony. Garrett laughed as he remembered telling Stephen all that time ago that the newcomer would never even see his room. How happy he was to be wrong. He delighted in the feel of his love snuggled close to him, looking up at the stars on such a clear night. Her hair glistened in the moonlight, but he noticed her eyes wore a troubled expression.

"What's on your mind tonight? You haven't said much since Jane and Henry left. Did something happen while they were here?"

Elise laid her head on his shoulder, craving the comfort of his arms. She let out a long sign before speaking softly. "Jane told me today what to do if the baby comes before she gets here. Hazel told me about what happened with Stephen's mother, and I'm just so afraid something will go wrong."

Garrett had heard the stories of things going wrong in childbirth, but he had to believe that wouldn't happen to his friends. He knew Elise had attended a few births in her time as a servant and knew she would know what to do if needed. "Doesn't it make you feel better, to be more prepared?"

She nodded her head a bit, but he could tell she wasn't convinced. "I just keep thinking that when the time comes, I won't know what to do."

"I know you will, you will be exactly what Christina will need, and you will know just what to do." He kissed her forehead and she smiled up at him.

"You have so much faith in me, Garrett," she looked out into the fields, then turned her eyes upwards to the glistening night sky, "I just wish I had some faith in myself."

The coming weeks passed with anticipation. Christina grew larger and more tired, ready to welcome her firstborn into the world. She spent many evenings with Stephen in his study, making plans for his coronation and their upcoming move into the castle. They were both so accustomed to living a royal lifestyle that the Manor had begun feeling cramped, and they longed for the day when Stephen's family home would be filled with a large and happy family.

"You should have been made King over a year ago." His wife mentioned one evening.

Stephen looked at her from his desk. "I suppose you're right, but so many things happened, and I kept waiting until it was the right time."

"I think if we spend our lives waiting for the right time, nothing will ever happen." She smiled at him, and he laughed.

"That's probably true. I had originally planned to wait only a couple of months, but then Elise came here, and you and I found each other, and then Garrett left and…." His voice grew shallow as he allowed himself to finally say the words, "…I didn't want to be alone. I knew if I took the thrown without a family by my side, I wouldn't be the King my father had raised me to be."

He looked down at the floor, feeling exposed, and vulnerable. Christina gently placed her hands on his shoulders and spoke words of assurance to her husband.

"You are a better man, and will be an even greater King, than he could have possibly dreamed, even if you had been alone in it. Stephen, I know that your father is so very proud of you. You didn't need us to become what you were born to be, but I'm so glad I get to be here to watch you reach it."

He put his arms around her and kissed her softly, his voice shaky from her generous words. "Thank you, my love."

Chapter Eighteen

It was early one summer morning, not quite dawn. Stephen dressed quietly and made his way out to the stables. He found Jones and requested his horse to be made ready, then headed out to do something very important.

Today would have been his father's 50Th birthday. He rode his horse slowly to the king's grave, noticing how his father's land was so lush and vibrant this year. He knew he would have been proud. He stood silently for some time, staring at his tombstone. Their family gravesite was far away from anywhere, out here in the countryside where they could rest in peace.

"Father," he began, "I miss you, so much. I have so many things that I want to tell you, questions I want to ask. I wish you could have met your daughter. I know you were ashamed to tell me about her, but I'm so glad you did. You would have loved her, just as much as I love her. Thank you for bringing her into my life, as well as Garrett. You knew so long ago that I would be left alone someday, and yet you filled my life with people that were there for me when I needed them the most."

Clouds began to roll in, lessening the morning light. He closed his eyes and pictured his father. "I wish you could have met Christina. I never knew what love truly was until I met her. We seem to know what the other is thinking all the time. She is full of so much joy and wisdom. When I think of what mother was like, I think she must have been just like her, and I know now how hard it was to lose her. I know about you leaving, but I want you to know that I forgive you. You came back and turned me into the man I am today, and I will never stop being grateful to you for that. I can only hope that I can guide my children the same way."

He heard the sound of thunder and opened his eyes. The wind began to blow and lightning flashed across the sky, Stephen felt a chill as the temperature dropped, and he knew he needed to leave. Walking back to his horse, he grabbed the reins and tried to mount, but the horse was spooked from the incoming storm.

"It must be a big one." He said to himself. He looked about the area and spotted a cave. Feeling it would be better to wait it out than to be caught in the storm, he pulled his horse under a tree and headed for shelter.

Garrett had just come back from a short ride with Raven when Jones came out to meet him. "It looks like a big storm is on its way, sir, I've almost finished securing down the horses."

He dismounted and passed the reigns to him. "Good idea, I'll help you finish." He walked into the stables and noticed another horse was missing. "Jones, where is Goldie?" The blonde horse was meant for Stephen, as a bribe to get him to go riding with Garrett. It seldom worked.

Jonas walked over to the empty pen. "My master took her out almost an hour ago."

Stephen was an adequate horseman, but preferred traveling by carriage. This news surprised him. "Did he say where he was going?"

He shook his head. "No, sir."

By now, the wind was blowing hard and thunder was rumbling the ground.

Elise walked around her parlor, singing softly and waiting for Christina. This was the usual time she would come in for a chat. She had been feeling tired lately, and Elise wondered if she was resting. An eerie feeling of urgency came over to her, and she turned and walked swiftly to her sister's room.

She reached the door when she heard a soft moaning noise. Elise knocked lightly, then turned the handle to peek inside. "Christina?" She whispered. "Are you alright?"

What she saw next confirmed her worries. Christina was leaning on her bedposts, her brow drenched in sweat and her face held in a painful grimace. The pain ended and she looked up at her sister, relieved that she was here now. "Oh, Elise, I'm so glad you came! I was sleeping when this terrible pain woke me."

She rushed to her side. "Why didn't you send for someone?"

She helped her to sit down on the bed and gently laid her back on her pillows. "At first, I thought he was just kicking me, but then it got so bad I couldn't walk over to the bell."

Elise felt her sister's stomach. The baby was much lower than he was before. The pain returned and Elise wisely placed both hands on her belly and felt the contraction. "It's alright, I'm here with you now."

The pain eased and Christina looked up at her sister's face. "The baby is coming."

The wind and rain howled outside of the cave Stephen had taken shelter in. He was warm enough, but stuck here until it passed. He had no idea the storm would be this big or last as long. Sitting down on a rock, he let out a long sigh. "Today of all days" he said to himself. He knew today would be bleak, but this? He certainly didn't expect to be trapped in a cave by his father's grave site. "Well, at least it can't get any worse."

No sooner than he said those words, that lightning struck a nearby tree down and completely blocked the entrance of the cave.

"Let's get you a little more comfortable." Elise helped her sister change out of her morning dress and into a loose nightgown. Another contraction overcame her and she held onto Elise's hand until it had eased. Once she was able to move, Elise guided her slowly back to bed. Christina noticed that Elise had lined the bed with extra linens.

"I am so glad you are here with me! I don't know what I would have done."

Elise helped her sit at the edge of the bed and then sat down next to her. "I'm not going anywhere, don't you worry. I do think it's time that we send for the midwife, I'll just go and ring the bell and I will be right back."

She got up quickly, her heart beating fast. Once the midwife got here, Elise knew everything would be alright. Before she could ring the bell, there was a knock. She opened the bedroom door to find Garrett, soaking wet and breathing hard. Elise looked back at Christine, then closed the door slightly.

"What's happened? Why are you all wet?" She whispered.

Garrett ran his hand quickly over his head. "There's a big storm that just settled over us, it looks bad. I helped Jones get the horses secured but it started raining hard before we could get in." He looked over her shoulder and saw Christina sitting on the bed in her night clothes. "Is she alright?"

Elise kept her voice low, as not to worry anyone. "The baby is coming. I need you to get Stephen and send for the midwife, right away."

Garrett's eyes looked uncertain. "Stephen's not here, and the storm is too bad to send for help."

"What?? Where is he?" She started to panic.

"I don't know, they said he took Goldie and left over an hour ago, but nobody knows where."

Elise pondered the words he spoke. "Well, if Stephen is gone and the midwife can't get here yet, send for Hazel. She will know what to do."

Garrett nodded his head and quickly took off toward the servant's quarters. Elise closed the door and said a quick prayer before going back to her sister's side. She rubbed her back through another contraction. "Somethings wrong, isn't it?" She asked.

Elise didn't want her to worry, but she knew it was better to tell her now instead of later. "There's a bad storm over us right now. Garrett said it's too bad to send for help."

Christina sighed and nodded her head. "Oh, well that's not so bad. I have you here and Stephan can help us."

Elise bit her bottom lip and Christina knew there was more. "Stephen went out riding and no one knows where."

"Oh no, I forgot, I was supposed to tell you. Today was the late king's birthday. He went to his father's grave."

"Oh, I didn't realize." That meant it had been well over a year since she came to live here. How much has changed in that time. "I've sent Garrett for Hazel, she will know what to do."

Another contraction came over her, but this one was different. Christina moaned loudly and then grabbed her sister's arm. "Something's happened…"

Elise helped her sister lean back into bed and lifted her nightgown. There was a small amount of blood. She remembered the first time she had seen this, and the midwife had explained to her that it was a sign the baby would be born soon. She put her nightgown back down and told her sister everything was perfectly fine, but now she needed to rest.

There was a hurried knock at the door and Olivia came in. "Pardon me, ma'am. Hazel is visiting her friend in the village today. Garrett sent me to see what I could do for you.

For one, slight moment, Elise felt her heart stop. No Stephen, no midwife, no Hazel. She was the only one here who could help this baby to be born. Christina was hit with another contraction and suddenly Elise knew what they needed to do. She directed Olivia to gather supplies.

"We will need plenty of hot water, extra linens, and several basins. Oh, and go to the kitchen to get a small knife and some twine." Olive nodded and ran to get the things.

Garrett opened the door slightly and called for Elise. "What can I do?"

Christina moaned loudly in pain, then recovering from the contraction, she looked at him. "I need my husband, Garrett. Please bring him to me!"

"He's at the king's gravesite." Elise informed him. "Is it far from here?"

Garrett shook his head. "No, it isn't far, but I won't be able to get a horse out, I will have to walk."

She took on a worried expression, remembering the last time he had traveled through the pouring rain. "Be careful."

He nodded his head and then disappeared.

Elise turned her attention back to her sister. "I'm afraid it's just going to be us, Christina."

Her sister smiled weakly through the pain. "I feel safer knowing you are here, I know we can do this."

Garrett ran to his room and gathered some supplies into a leather bag. Not knowing what he would find, he brought a rope, a blanket, compass, and his pocket knife. He secured the bag to his back and then draped Henry's cloak around his shoulders before leaving.

Stephen tried everything he could to free himself from the cave, but nothing worked. The tree was too big to move from the inside. He sat back down in defeat, angry at himself. Putting his head down in his hands, he felt so weak. Suddenly, a voice came from the wind.

"Stephen, my son."

The prince felt the hair on the back of his neck stand up. No, it couldn't be.

"Stephen" the voice repeated.

This time, there was no mistaking it. The faint voice of his father was somehow speaking to him from beyond the grave.

"Father?"

"My son, I'm here. Don't be afraid."

Back at the Manor, Elise was keeping careful watch over her sister. She was getting very tired, so Olivia brought them all cups of strong tea and toast. It was important for Christina to keep her strength up.

"Do you think they are ok?" Christina was growing fearful over the whereabouts of her husband.

Elise wiped her sister's brow with a cool washcloth. "Better than that, I know they are ok."

Christina put her hands behind her lower back and groaned. "I hope you're right."

"Does your back hurt?" She asked suspiciously.

She braced herself for her next contraction, breathing the way Elise showed her, it helped get through the moment. "Yes, just constantly now."

Elise went to her sister and felt around her belly. She could tell from the baby's position and the pain in her back that the baby had his head turned. He also hadn't gone any lower into her pelvis.

"Christina, let's try to relieve some of that pressure. Can you get down on your hands and knees?"

"I'll try, if you think it will help." Olivia and Elise helped her get down, then they put a warmed towel over her lower back to give her some relief. Elise knelt down and rubbed her stomach, trying to get the baby to turn into a better position. They guided her through several contractions in this position, and then helped her stand up. Christina gasped as she felt something pop, and Elise announced it was her water breaking.

The baby was much lower now and her back pain was gone, that let her know it was almost time. They helped her back into bed and laid her down with several pillows behind her head. The next contraction she had, Elise saw her start to bear down and she told her it was time to push.

Garrett pushed through the wind and rain, hardly knowing where anything was. All he could think of was finding his friend. When Elise told him he was at his father's gravesite, he realized what day it was. He should have remembered, he should have gone with him. He heard a horse just ahead of him and followed the sound.

"Stephen!" He called out.

Finally, he found Goldie, the horses reigns tangled in a fallen tree. The rain began to subside as he approached the horse. "It's alright, girl, it's alright." He placed his hands gently on the horse, calming her. They were under a thick cover of trees that must have sheltered the horse through most of the storm. "Where's Stephen?" He asked the horse. He must be here somewhere. Garrett looked at the fallen tree and noticed something behind it. Clearing some of the branches with his knife, he climbed to the top of the tree and peered into the cave.

"There you are," he saw Stephen, passed out on the ground. He looked down at the tree beneath him. "Goldie, we have to move this tree." He took off his bag and retrieved the rope, tying it first around a thick branch, and then to Goldie's saddle. Garrett walked around to the front of the horse and grasped her reigns in his hands. "Alright now, on three," he braced his feet against the ground, twisted the reigns around his wrists, and stood ready to pull." One…two…three!"

The horse pulled hard and the tree moved a good foot out of the way. Two more pulls and it was free enough for Garrett to get inside. He climbed in and went to his friend. Checking his pulse, he was relieved to find he was still alive. "Tree must have knocked you out when it fell." He felt a bump on his head but otherwise he seemed fine. "Wake up, Stephen."

"I can't do this any longer!" Christina was exhausted from labor, she had been pushing for what seemed like forever.

Elise knew the end was very near. "Yes you can, I can see his head! Just a few more pushes and your baby will be here!"

Christina shook her head and sobbed. "I need Stephen, I need my husband!"

Elise was worried about Garrett as well, but they had to get through this before they could think about them. Another contraction came and Christina pushed as hard as she could, wanting so badly for it to be over.

"What…what's going on?" Stephen was groggy and disoriented when Garrett woke him up.

"You're alright, you just got knocked out when the tree fell." Garrett was helping him up to his feet slowly.

The prince looked at the tree. "I thought….I thought my father…"

"You should have told me what day it was, I would have come with you."

Shaking the confusion from his mind, his eyes began to focus. "I know, my friend, I know. I just needed to talk to him for a while, father to son."

Garrett brought the blanket out from his pack and draped it over Stephens's shoulders. He helped him mount the horse and then took the reins to guide her. "Let's get you home."

Christina held her newborn son in her arms, wrapped in the blanket she had knitted for him, and marveled at how beautiful he was. Elise and Olivia cleaned up the room, smiling at the safe delivery of the healthy young prince.

"Just wait until he sees you," she kissed his tiny hands and looked up at Elise. "I wonder where they could be."

Elise had allowed herself to worry now, and imagined the worst. Thankfully, their fears were short lived. Garrett opened the door slightly and peeked his head in. "Hello?"

Elise ran to the door and opened it wide, she threw her arms around him in spite of the fact that he was again drenched in rain. "I'm so happy you're back! Did you find him?"

Garrett stepped aside to allow Stephen into the room. Garrett hadn't said a word about what was going on, wishing to surprise his friend with the happy news. The look of shock and sheer joy on his face brought tears to all of their eyes. "Darling," his wife reached for him and he went to her side, "we have a son."

Elise, Garrett, and Olivia stepped out to let the new family bond. Elise hugged her assistant and thanked her for coming to help, then turned to Garrett and melted into his arms. He held her tight as she started to cry.

"I was so scared, Garrett! I didn't know what I was going to do or what was going to happen. If I had lost her, or the baby, or you…"

He held her close. "But you didn't lose anyone, don't you see? You brought that baby safely into the world, when no one else could! You kept Christina calm and focused so she could do what she needed to do. You are amazing!"

She stopped crying, looked up at him, and smiled. That's exactly what she needed to here.

They heard a knock at the front door and Jane came in. She looked at Elise and Garrett. "Did the baby come?"

"Just now," Garrett told her. "How did you know to come?"

Jane smiled brightly. "I've been through enough storms in my day to know when a baby is going to make an appearance. I was in the carriage as soon as it started to subside. Where are they?"

Elise pointed to the room the new family was resting in, and Jane marched in, closing the door behind her.

"Come on, I need to get dry clothes on and you need to rest." He walked her to her room and she was grateful for a few moments of stillness.

Fifteen minutes later, Garrett walked out of his room and found Jones. He gave him instructions to bring several warm blankets and a basin of hot water to the prince's room. Stephen took the items gladly, grateful to warm up after the ordeal he had been through. Jane has just finished checking on Christina and the baby, pleased to report a perfect birth, thanks to Elise.

"How's the head?" He asked his friend.

"It'll heal. Come and meet your nephew!" Stephen whispered as not to upset the precious new baby. They walked over to the new mother and child, Christina's face, glowing. She raised the child up to Garrett and he stooped down to receive him.

"What's his name?" Garrett asked as he held the infants tiny hand.

Stephen glanced at his wife, and she nodded her approval. "Allow me to introduce Prince George."

Garrett held the baby close and whispered, "Named after your grandfather and born on his birthday? Now that's something worth celebrating!"

Elise changed her clothes and went to her bed, but her mind was too full to sleep. She thought back over the eventful day, first feeling nothing but terror, then finding the confidence to do what need to be done. Elation took over her thoughts. "I delivered a baby today," she said to herself. Realization took over her, and her whole body began to shake. She felt powerful, alive. She was part of something that was bigger than anything in her past. A brief knock at her door caused her to stir just before it opened, and Jane came inside, beaming with pride at her friend.

"Elise!" She shrieked as she went quickly to her bedside.

She sat up, swung her legs over the bed, and opened her arms to welcome the one person in her life that would understand how she was feeling. "Jane! I don't even know what to say!"

Happy tears misted her eyes. "I know, dear, oh, how I know!"

Elise began to sob uncontrollably. She held her friend, wisely allowing her to release everything she was feeling. When her tears were spent, she sat up and dried her eyes.

"Is this how you feel?" She asked.

Jane smiled at her friend. "Oh yes. Especially the first few times. You feel more and more confident each time, and then you can use those feelings when you need them. When it's the dead of night and you have just returned from a long and tedious birth, just to be called out to another laboring mother, or when you have to make a decision to save a life and you aren't sure what to do, you draw on those feelings to get you through it." Janes face clouded over with pain, and she spoke her next words softly. "Or if you have to look into the eyes of a new mother, just to tell her that her baby was born sleeping….."

Jane's voice trailed off for a moment, before rallying. "But that was not the case today!"

Elise felt herself shudder, so very thankful that her friend was right. "No, thank God, it was not."

Chapter Nineteen

Weeks later, Elise and Garrett called a family meeting. Christina sat comfortably on the sofa, nursing her newborn son, wrapped in the silky blanket she had worked so hard on. Stephen sat at his desk, Elise and Garrett in the chairs opposite.

"We've given this a lot of thought, and we wanted to let you know our decision." Garrett began, holding his beloved's hand for support.

Stephen raised an eyebrow, unsure of what news his friend was planning to share.

Elise spoke next. "Stephen, I can't tell you how grateful I am to you. You rescued me from a nightmare and brought me to this beautiful home. Highfield has become a place of joy, and will always hold a special place in both of our hearts. I want you to know that I will always be your sister, but I have decided not to claim a position in the royal line."

Stephen looked shocked, alarmed. "What, what do you mean? You don't want to be part of the family?"

Elise shook her head, "Of course I want to be part of the family, I love you very much, and I told you I will always be your sister, no matter what." She paused a moment, trying to find the words. "Garrett and I have decided not to claim a royal title. We wish to live a quiet, simple life in the village."

Elise and Garrett looked at each other, eyes shining. They were thrilled to start this new life with each other.

"I must say, I was not expecting this. Where do you plan to live? Not far away, I hope?"

It was time now for Garrett to disclose the fortune he had been left. He told them about the house his Uncle had purchased in Westmore village, and their plans to move there permanently after they were married.

Christina laid her sleeping son in a tiny cot and walked over to them. "What can we do to help you start your journey?"

Garrett glanced at Stephen, and he nodded in agreement. "Anything for you, brother."

"Well, we would like to move our horses to the new estate, if that's alright" He had arranged for Autumn, the horse from Mournstead, to be brought to Highfield for Elise.

"They are your horses, Garrett, of course you can take them with you." He smiled at such a simple request. "Tell me, what do you both intent to do with your time?"

It was time now for Elise to share. "Jane has offered to teach me to be a midwife. The village is growing, and is too much for her to keep up with on her own; plus she says I have a natural talent."

Christina put her hand on her sister's shoulder. "I completely agree."

She was grateful for her kind words of assurance. "And Garrett will raise horses." She exclaimed proudly.

"Horses and children?" Stephen joked.

Elise and Garrett laughed. "Whatever we are blessed with, my friend."

Once Christina and baby George were well enough to travel, the five of them went into the village to see the house that Garrett's uncle had left him.

"Why do you think he bought it?" Stephen asked him.

"I've been wondering that myself." He said truthfully. "I believe he had found his fortune and wanted to come back here to make amends with me. He was captain of his own ship, and had told several of his crewmates about me and the life he had walked away from. I think he regretted leaving so soon."

They arrived at the estate. It was smaller than Highfield, but easily the largest home in the village. It was close enough to town that Elise could be summoned at any time, but far enough away to be a quiet place for the horses.

Garrett noticed a sign above the door, and called out for Elise to see it.

"Rosewood View" the plaque stated. The house was perfectly named, for roses had a special place in their hearts.

They looked at each other, smiling at this new chapter in their lives. This house held the promise of a new beginning. It would be a place of hope, for living life to the fullest, and for real, honest love. They went inside and toured every room, Elise and Christina planning what each one would be used for, but it wasn't until they saw the view from the back parlor window that they knew they were home.

A garden of vibrant red rose bushes surrounded the back of the estate, with paths intertwining with each other, leading to a patch of forest that simply begged to be explored. They felt instantly connected to this place. Garrett pictured he and Elise taking Raven and Autumn on a trip through the forest, discovering all of the secrets it held, while Elise could see them having breakfast out in the rose garden, like they did that day on her balcony.

Stephen gathered his tiny son into his arms and showed him around the new home. "This, Georgie, is your Aunt and Uncle's new home. I want you to get a real good look at it, because I'm sure you will be spending lots of time here. Uncle Garrett will give you a horse and teach you how to ride, and Aunt Elise will stuff you full of goodies and give you everything you ask for, won't she?"

He gave a sly grin to his sister who couldn't help but laugh. "Only if he behaves, isn't that right George?"

The baby cooed and gurgled in agreement.

"Stephen," Garrett called out. "What do you intend to do with the Manor? Close it off?" He knew they were going to move into the castle permanently once they were married.

"Christina and I have talked about that," Stephen placed his son into the ready arms of his wife, "we plan on keeping it ready and open for visiting. We may not be able to spend whole summers together anymore, but hopefully we can all be together often enough."

Garrett and Elise went back to the new house often, making arrangements, ordering furniture, and planning their dreams. Soon everything would be ready and they could start their new lives together. In the meantime, Elise spent time catching up with Grace, and learning midwifery from Jane. She had become just as much Elise's friend as she was Garrett's, and he couldn't be more pleased.

Once their new home was almost finished, they announced that it was time to begin wedding preparations. Christina hired a dressmaker to come to the Manor and design a wedding gown for her friend. She was delighted to share in the planning, as her own wedding had happened so fast.

"It was like a fairy tale" she told Elise, when retelling the story of her whirlwind romance. "As soon as I first saw him, I knew there was a spark. He seemed to know just what I was thinking. When I asked my father to extend the invitation to our kingdom, I hardly dared hope that he would agree, then when we received word immediately that he had accepted, I knew he felt the same way."

"When did you know he was The One?" Elise wondered.

"Honestly, and he will tell you a different story, but I knew sometime during that first visit." Christina sat in a lounge chair, cradling her handsome son. "We were at a party, and he had asked me to dance. I enjoyed his company, surely, but what I noticed was how he danced with me verses how he danced with other girls. When he danced with them, it seemed as though he couldn't wait until it was over, but when he danced with me, it was like he didn't want it to stop. That's when I knew I loved him."

"Why would he tell me it happened at another time?" Elise asked as she rummaged through the selections the dressmaker had brought.

Christina smiled at the memory. "Because he thinks the moment I fell in love with him was at the end of his second visit."

"Why does he think that?" She asked.

"Well, the moment he thinks it happened, was actually just the moment I let him see it. We were touring the countryside and he told me he was leaving to go back home soon. I told him I wished he could stay, and so we made the short tour last as long as possible. We didn't go back to my home until dusk, and then I let him kiss me in the light of the sunset when it was time to say goodbye. That's when he thinks it happened."

Christina glowed at the retelling of her story. Elise was lost in the romance of it all. "What was the wedding like?"

"Well, we didn't have much time, it was only days after he proposed. Our priest was escorted to our castle, and my brother's family luckily were already there. My mother had saved her wedding gown that I had always wanted to use, and Stephen had the rings. We had the ceremony in our main hall, and it was beautiful. I felt like I was on an adventure, and I couldn't wait to see what life had in store for us. I haven't been disappointed in the least." She kissed the hand of her sweet baby, her eyes, glowing with love. "I know it will be the same for you, sister."

The dressmaker arrived and set everything up in the same room she had been in over a year ago when she had her first dresses made. Going through this experience again made her remember the feelings she had the first time. Like Christina, that was the moment that she knew, the moment she first allowed herself to not only admit her feelings, but to explore and act on them. She now understood that this was also the moment that she first became more than what she had been. On that day, fear and unworthiness, doubt and self-loathing, they had begun to slip away, and a new person was taking form. Not a scared little girl, but a confident young woman, who knew what she wanted out of life, and had the means to take it. That was the day she discovered that she had the power to make a better life for herself.

The dress was finished and Elise stepped out to show her sister, whose eyes welled up with tears at the sight of her.

"Oh Elise, its perfect!"

Garrett had taken Stephen with him to the tailor's shop to have his suit made for the wedding. He had first thought Elise would have wanted a quiet, private ceremony, but she surprised him with plans of something much grander.

Garrett was happy to have his best friend by his side again. It felt good to share these moments with him.

"You know, when I was in Mournstead, I remember thinking that all the plans I had for the village, they reminded me of you."

Stephen raised an eyebrow. "How so?"

"You've always done things so meticulously. You make a plan, patiently wait through each and every step, and then finally, the satisfaction comes from knowing the job was done right. Sometimes, I envied that about you, but then I realized, it's exactly what I was doing there. It was tedious work, but once it was finished, I felt that same satisfaction. It was almost like a part of you was there with me, telling me what I should do." Garrett's voice was low, trying to keep his emotions in check with his heartfelt speech.

Stephen appreciated his words more than Garrett would ever know. "It's funny you would say that, actually." He sat down in a chair a few feet away from where Garrett was standing. "When I went to see Christina that last time before you left, I was going through so many emotions. I knew what I wanted and I didn't want to wait for it. For the first time in my life, I didn't make a big plan, I didn't sit and calculate the steps, I just knew what I wanted and I reached for it. You've always been so passionate and assured with everything you've done, and for a long time, I wondered what it must be like to live life so fearlessly. I think a part of you was with me, as well."

"Maybe that's not such a bad thing, for either of us. I can see that I've started to slow down, think things through, and you've really begun to let go and embrace the good things in your life." Garrett turned his head toward Stephen. "He would have been so proud of you, and who you have become."

Stephen nodded his head slowly, a smile beginning to form across his face. "He would have been proud, of both of us."

Chapter Twenty

A week before the wedding, the Manor seemed to buzz with excitement. The servants bustled around the grounds making preparations, the ladies of the house made countless plans and gave all manner of instructions, while the men simply tried to make sense of it all.

"Elise, what is all of this fuss?" Garrett would tease. "I don't care about silks or feathers or whatever else you and Christina have planned, I just want to marry you." He held her tightly in his arms, and she reveled in the feeling of his returned strength.

His fiancé laughed at his playful banter. "We only have one more week, surely we can wait just a little longer?"

Her flirtatious tone reminded him that in only a week, he was going to live in a new home with his bride; all those months of hardship, agony, and loneliness would soon fade away, and all that would be left of it would be a faint memory. She would be his and he would be hers, and no one would ever take that away. He leaned forward and placed his forehead on hers, wishing the time away. "Just one more week."

That night, the four of them sat in the parlor after dinner, talking over future plans.

"Do you know," spoke Elise to her brother, "In all my time here, I've never seen the castle?"

Stephen looked incredulous. "Really? Have we never taken you there?"

She shook her head. "You and Garrett talk about it so much, you plan to live there permanently, and I know you and Christina have made several trips, yet I've never seen it."

"Well," Stephen announced to the room, "Why don't we go and see it then?"

"Oh yes!" Christina clapped. "Let's have a visit before the wedding."

And so the next day they made a trip up to the castle. It was much larger than Elise had imagined, but the rest of the group seemed un-phased, as though it was perfectly normal.

"Garrett," she whispered before going inside, "You didn't tell me it was so big!"

He chuckled and offered her his arm. "I was intimidated when I first saw it too. Just remember that before the king became ill, this was our home most of the time, the Manor was just for summers and vacations. It's not so bad once you get used to it."

He showed her each of the main rooms, pointing out his favorite parts and telling her stories from his childhood. She was so intimidated by the luxury the castle had in every inch of its interior, and was never so happy that she decided not to claim a title. The Manor was the grandest place she had ever seen, but to live here? This was beyond her comfort.

They finished the tour, ate lunch in one of the main rooms, and then went back to Highfield. Garrett felt a change come over Elise, and he asked her to take a walk with him to the stables. They walked in silence until they arrived. "I know something is on your mind, please tell me." He spoke with such gentleness, she couldn't help but confide in him.

"Garrett, you told me it was my choice whether or not we would claim a title in the royal family."

He didn't know where this was going. "Yes."

"And I chose not to." Her voice became a bit shaky, and he feared she was having second thoughts about their future together. He placed her hands into his and she leaned into him.

"Elise, are you regretting that decision? Are you regretting....?" His voice trailed off, but it sounded fearful.

She was quick to put his mind at ease. "No, I'm not regretting the choices I've made. I want to marry you and live in our beautiful home and make a life with you. But today, at the castle, knowing how you were raised, it made me wonder if that choice was holding you back from a better life."

"Better? What do you mean?" He searched her eyes for an explanation.

"I don't want my choice to live a simple life to mean that you can't live the life you are accustomed to." She turned away from him, not knowing what he would say next.

Garrett thought about her words briefly before gently turning her back to face him. "I told you it was your choice because I would have been happy either way."

"But if I had chosen a title, your life would be like what you had." She tried to explain her feelings to him.

"Elise, I understand what you are saying. It was the reason I left in the first place. I loved you enough to let you go, so that you could have more than what I could offer you. But please understand, the life I lived in that castle wasn't mine, it was Stephens. I was happy to live it alongside him for that time, but I lived it as a servant, not as a royal. If that was the life you had chosen, I would have accepted it, but it wasn't what I really wanted."

He held her close to his heart, trying to show just how much she meant to him. "I want to spend my life with you, in our own house, with our own rules, making our own choices. If you had chosen a title, I would have sacrificed that dream for you, and I still will, if that is what you truly want."

Knowing that he wanted the same life that she did made her feel so much closer to him. "No, I don't want that at all. I want our own life too."

He breathed a heavy sigh of relief. "Then, I have something for you." He reached into his pocket and pulled out a small black bag, handing it to her.

She opened the top and turned the bag over, allowing its contents to slip into her hand. A delicate silver necklace fell out of the bag, and she turned it over until she saw her mother's dove pendant. She gasped, tears filling her eyes.

Garrett picked the necklace up out of her hands and placed it around her neck. "You've made a choice now, to live by your own rules, and to make your own life. With me, or without, you are free."

They stayed for a while in the stables, then walked back to the Manor together, their view of the future clearer than ever.

Christina walked into Elise's parlor carrying her child. Garrett stood by the fireplace waiting for his beloved to arrive.

"Guess who woke up from his nap?" She asked whimsically as Garrett reached out for him.

"Let me see my handsome nephew, so I can tell him all about his new horse." Elise helped him pick a young mare, who now resided at the new stables at Rosewood.

Christina gently placed her child in the loving arms of his soon-to-be uncle. "There you go, George Patrick."

"I understand 'Patrick' is a family name, from your side?" He questioned while slowly rocking the baby in his arms.

For one brief moment, Christina's face lost the joy it usually held. "Yes, that's right, after my brother."

Garrett turned this over in his mind. "I thought your brother's name was William?"

"My older brother, yes, but Patrick was the name of my younger brother."

He picked up the saddened tone in her voice, and proceeded with caution. "Was?"

She looked down at the floor and took a deep breath, then shook her head as if to banish painful memories. "He passed away, when we were both very young."

"I'm so sorry, I had no idea."

"Thank you. I suppose that's my fault, I don't talk about him as much as I should."

A moment of silence passed between them before Garrett continued. "What happened, if I may ask?"

She held a faraway expression, "My father's kingdom is near the sea. We used to go sea-bathing in the summer months when we were little. Patrick was two years younger than me, and I was very fond of him." Christina looked into the fire, her eyes glazing over with memories of the past. "It was windy that day, the waves were much larger than normal, and my parents warned us not to go into the water. Something must have caught his eye, and he turned and ran straight into the waves. By the time my father got him out, it was too late."

He didn't know what to say. How tragic to lose a sibling. Garrett's uncle came to his mind, and he wondered if the water had taken his life, too.

He stood up and placed the baby in his mother's lap, then gave his sister-in-law a comforting hug, feeling closer to her now. She allowed a few tears to escape her eyes as she laid her head on his shoulder.

Elise came into the room, saw the pair grieving, and became alarmed. "What's happened?"

Christina picked up her head and dried her tears on her handkerchief. "I was just telling him about my brother, Patrick."

She placed her hand over her sisters, and Garrett realized that Elise already knew the story. He remembered they had several months to get to know each other before he came back.

"I know he would have been proud to have his nephew named after him, he will not be forgotten."

"Thank you, Garrett. You are too kind."

Their wedding day had finally arrived. The early fall garden had been arranged with enough room for what seemed like the entire village. Grace and Jane's families had reserved seats of honor, along with Florence, Clara, and baby Christopher. Elise wanted to show the world how happy she was to marry her soulmate. White chairs, a flowering arch, and a path of rose petals patiently waited for their moment to shine. The grand hall had been set up for a light dinner reception; the room that had been so intimidating to her would now welcome her guests with joy.

Christina sat with Elise in her room while Hazel and Olivia fastened their hair. The sisters wanted to get ready together, knowing this was the last day they would live at Highfield.

"I remember when you first came to us, Miss." Hazel was brushing out Elise's long hair in front of the mirror like she had on that first day. "You have changed so much since then."

Elise reached her hand up to touch Hazel's. "I certainly feel different. I remember being afraid to touch anything in this room."

Christina began, "Just think of how it would have been if Stephen's father had only known about you from the start."

"I do think about that sometimes, how different my life would have been."

Olivia was carefully arranging Christina's blonde curls. "You would have grown up in the castle with Stephen and Garrett."

Elise tried to picture a life raised by the father she never knew. Instead of being a lowly servant, she would have had servants of her own. Her days would have been spent learning to be a proper princess, with lessons and etiquette.

"I don't think Garrett and I would have had the same relationship if we had grown up together. Stephen was right to conceal the truth from him for as long as he did." Elise glanced at her sister. "I think he would have put up a wall between us, thinking he wasn't good enough."

"Do you think you would have thought so, too?" Christina asked.

"I certainly hope not, in fact, I sometimes think the opposite, that I'm not good enough for him. When I think of how selflessly he devoted himself to improving the lives of the children and servants in Mournstead, I'm just so in awe of his goodness."

Christina's hair was finished, and she got up to walk over to her sisters table. "What about the girl who agreed to marry a stranger, to honor the wishes of the man she really loved? I'd say that was pretty selfless."

She thanked and hugged her sister, grateful for her presence and her kind words. Hazel finished with her hair, then she and Olivia brought out her wedding gown. They lovingly placed and fastened the dress, custom made to fit her flawlessly.

Elise turned to face the mirror, and they all gasped. She looked like the image she had carried in her mind of her mother.

"You look like an angel, Miss, a true princess." Hazel declared as her eyes began to mist.

"No," Christina said, smiling at her sister, knowing that wasn't what she wanted for herself. "She looks like a bride."

In the warm sunshine of the autumn afternoon, Elise and Garrett were married. The ceremony was held in the courtyard of Highfield Manor. Roses and candles lined the walkway that Elise walked down, toward the man she loved more than anything. Once a scared, hurting young woman, she was now a beloved friend, sister, and soon, a wife. She treasured the time she had spent here, even the struggles and mistakes made along the way, because they made her who she was today. A strong, confidant woman, loved by a family she never knew she could have. As she walked down towards her future husband, she knew who she was, and she knew what she wanted. She wanted this gift of a life she had been given. She wanted the man who stood waiting for her. Her future was bright and her path was clear. Her head was held high as she walked gracefully toward the rest of their lives.

-Epilogue-

The prince became first a father, and then a king. His coronation took place a few months after the wedding, and they now resided permanently in the castle. Christina beamed at her little family, she was so happy here. They quickly grew accustomed to their new surroundings. Knowing his family was near gave Stephen the confidence to lead his people the way his father had taught him to, with wisdom and kindness. Two years ago, he was alone. Scared for his future, and hopeless. Now he had such a large family that his heart could barely contain his joy. With a wife he loved and his child at his side, his long lost sister and new brother close by, he felt whole again. He knew, no matter what trials his life would hold, no matter what pain he would face, he would always have his family to draw strength and comfort from.

Made in the USA
Columbia, SC
02 February 2020

87431876R00115